Daisy
does it
Herself

CW01497631

Daisy does it Herself

GRACIE PLAYER

For Errol

Contents

One

Bloody British summer. It had been blue skies ahoy when we set out just a few minutes ago. Now the sky was scudding with black clouds and slinging down heavy sheets of rain.

It had been roasting for weeks, the fierce, clammy hot of a city heatwave. Far from having a cooling effect, the rain seemed to exacerbate the issue, pressing the air down like a steaming towel, smothering all of London in its folds. I blew a strand of sweaty hair off my forehead.

The air conditioning had not yet kicked in, and the inside of Phil's Mercedes ran with condensation. All in all, it was pretty hot and steamy in the car—and not in a good way.

Phil sat beside me in the passenger seat, his lips getting thinner and whiter with each passing moment. A bead of sweat inched out of his hairline and rolled down his face. I flipped the left indicator and took the corner at a sedate pace.

'I honestly don't know why you're putting yourself through this, Daisy love,' Phil said, his handsome face rearranging itself into an expression of concern. 'You've got a perfectly good chauffeur right here.' He doffed an imaginary cap in my direction.

'I know, babe,' I said, turning back to concentrate on the road, 'but I'm determined to pass this time around.' Three disastrous driving tests in, at the ripe old age of twenty-six, I was starting to doubt I would ever learn to drive.

I think Phil would have preferred it if I'd given up completely. But when I persisted, he insisted on teaching me himself. To be honest, his need to control everything could be a little wearing. But it's best to pick your battles, I guess. So here we were.

'Anyway, Ruby said she'll take me out as well, when she gets back, which should help.'

Phil made a non-committal harrumphing sound.

My best friend Ruby was currently *finding herself* after a particularly nasty breakup. Mainly by boinking her way across Southeast Asia.

Ruby and I had known each other forever, since the first day of primary school to be exact. Ruby – as kind and empathetic as she was bossy and occasionally thoughtless – had noticed the shy little church mouse that was my five-year-old self, cowering in the corner and decided then and there that that simply would not do. She actually said that, the precocious little diva.

I can still see her, hand on hip. Pretty face scrunched up into a frown. 'No babes,' she said, handing me a tissue. 'This simply won't do.' I took the tissue and blew my nose enthusiastically.

'What do you suggest?' I'd asked.

Which led to the first of many scrapes that Ruby was to get me into over the years. And this is how, on my first day of primary school, I got my first trip to the headmaster's office. And also my first and dearest friend.

Phil and Ruby had never seen eye to eye. Sometimes I thought Phil was a little jealous of our relationship, which was kind of cute, I guess. Though I hated the tension between the two most important people in my life. But Ruby, well, she'd never been afraid to speak her mind—let's put it that way. And wonderful as Phil was, accepting criticism had never been his strong suit. Not from Ruby, yours truly, or anybody else. Don't get me wrong, most of the time he was thoughtful and funny and loving. It was just that he had his pressure points, same as everyone else.

Up ahead, a flock of umbrellas, presumably with people underneath, swarmed towards the pedestrian crossing. I started to apply the brakes as the traffic lights changed to red. I managed the transition fairly smoothly, switching to first gear without looking down and pulling to a stop only a smidge over the line. 'Nice,' Phil said, and I turned and smiled at him, thinking how handsome he looked. Even when he was a hot, sweaty mess.

I absolutely adored Phil, despite the odd niggle, which was perfectly normal for any couple after years together, two of those cohabiting. I'm sure he harboured a few pet peeves about me too. To give one example, I knew for a fact it drove him mad when I went to the corner shop in my pyjamas. In my defence, they were very nice pyjamas, although the purple pom-pom slippers may have been a bit much. When Phil pointed this out, I swapped them for my Ugg boots. See, our relationship had its compromises, as all the best ones did.

Seriously though, he was actually pretty great. We met when I was just twenty, living in grotty shared accommodation with four unfriendly strangers and pulling pints in a wine bar up town.

One evening, this rowdy group of city blokes in pinstripe suits rolled in. Phil made a beeline straight for me. He asked me out that same night and I said yes. To be honest, I got asked out a lot in the wine bar, usually by utter knobheads or gentlemen of the elderly persuasion. I'd gotten pretty adept at brushing them off, egos intact. A hazard of the job.

But I couldn't believe that this sophisticated older man, with a plush job and a car and a posh suit, was interested in me. Phil was a bit of a dreamboat (my mother's words). A rugby player's build in a Gucci suit. Charm and swagger for days. Anyway, here we were six years later. And I still couldn't bloody drive.

I squinted and rubbed a circle on the steamy windscreen with the back of my hand. My hair, I noticed, was doing alarming things. I'd ruthlessly straightened it that morning and one side held dark, glossy and smooth while the other side seemed to have puffed up like a cotton candy ball. I blew at a strand that had stuck to my face and tried to fiddle with the windscreen wipers.

'No, no, silly, like this,' Phil said. 'Come on now, Goose, we've been through this,' he went on, using the cutesy pet name that I wouldn't dream of telling him I secretly hated. Like really, *really* hated.

'Get ready, Daisy,' Phil said as the lights changed from red to amber. I scrambled for the handbrake, the car jerked forward and we were off. I narrowly avoided ploughing through the centre of a puddle. Unfortunately, I caught it with my rear wheel and a pedestrian looked up in alarm as a mini tidal wave roared up and splattered him with muddy London rain. He jumped back shaking his fist and I mouthed 'Sorry,' into the mirror as I sped away. By this point we'd made it as far as the end of the block.

'Time to turn back then?' I asked cheerfully.

Phil nodded. 'I think that would be for the best, Goose,' he said, patting my leg.

Two

Sunday morning. I rolled over and covered my eyes with a groan. My stomach gave a little skip and I wondered for one, long, icky moment if I was going to throw up. To be honest, that seemed like a lot of fuss and effort. I decided against it and reluctantly cranked open my eyes instead.

Phil's side of the bed was empty. The freak must have got up early and gone to the gym. I was sort of glad he wasn't there to see me like this. He was one of those annoying people who could drink as much as they liked and it barely seemed to touch them. Consequently, he had little to no sympathy for mere mortals like me, who only had to sniff a drop of wine to be absolutely hanging the next day.

I swung my legs over the side of the bed and rustled around for my slippers. The world lurched for a moment, before deciding it wasn't going to punish me with too bad of a hangover. I said a little prayer of thanks to the booze gods and tottered off to the bathroom to have a wee and inspect the damage.

Oh Christ, I still had on my dress from last night. Wrapped around my neck to be precise. I must have tried to take it off before stumbling into bed and gotten myself tangled up in it.

Just how drunk was I?

'Daisy, you are a classy bird,' I muttered, untangling myself from the clutches of the dress before it throttled me and slinging the damn thing in the laundry basket with a curse.

Phil bought the dress for my birthday last year and, dare I say, it was a little slutty. Still, he liked me in it, so I made the effort to dust the shimmery, slinky item off once in a while. Though truth be told, it had always been a little on the snug side.

Hmm, maybe I should have gone to the gym after all. Phil always said it was nothing to do with weight, it was all about health, and I'd just feel all-round healthier if I worked out a little more. I thought that was a bit unfair. I wasn't a gym nut by any means, but I did go for jogs quite regularly. Admittedly, the last time I stepped into an actual gym I was climbing a rope in PE shorts.

I slouched downstairs in one of Phil's old T-shirts, looking like the Creature from the Black Lagoon and Swamp Thing made a baby. I didn't know how Phil managed it. All I wanted was Pepsi on a drip and carbs. Lots of carbs.

I poked around the fridge, looking for anything with a hint of fat to soak up the booze. But nope, Phil was up before eight and off to the gym and our fridge was full of lettuce. In the end I settled for toast and jam, which, it turned out, was just the thing. Three slices and a cup of tea later, I felt almost human again.

I sat sipping the last few inches of tea, listening to the radio and enjoying the me-time while pootling about on my iPad. I wiped my buttery fingers on a tea towel and navigated to an article about some new developments in SEO that I was interested in. Search Engine Optimisation, that is, to civilians; a highly technical bit of witchery that involves techniques for pushing a website higher up the results page in Google.

A year ago, I started as a temp, doing admin work for a small corporate event management company. My first office job. I was meant to be filing, doing data entry and making tea. Basically, all the crap jobs that nobody else wanted to do. But three weeks in, the managing director, a caustically sarcastic man named Oliver, had casually tasked me with managing the website, updating content and the like.

'The IT guy (I think most people in the office think that's his actual name) will show you the ropes,' he'd said, noticing my horrified expression. 'Oh, and Daisy dear, we'd like to see a ten percent increase in traffic to the website in, let's say, three months?'

What? I'd thought. *What did he just ask me to do? What the hell has traffic got to do with anything?*

'Think you can manage that?' he asked.

'Sure thing,' I'd said, beaming confidently, although I was quaking on the inside. Dear God, I didn't know the arse end of a computer from its elbow—or that computers have neither arses nor elbows, clearly.

But as it turned out, I had something of an aptitude for all things digital. Who knew! Not only did I improve web traffic, i.e. visitors to the website, by significantly more than ten percent, I introduced a few simple changes that meant our conversion rates went through the roof, leading to a big increase in leads and bookings.

Not that getting to that point was easy. Far from it. In a protracted, panic-induced fugue state, the first place I went was, ironically, the Internet. 'What is website traffic?' I typed into the search box and off I went down the rabbit hole.

I was surprised to find that, beyond all the trolling and Instagram models making perfectly normal people feel fat, the Internet could be a wonderful, generous place. It was actually a great leveller in some ways. My school education, in retrospect, was pretty shoddy and I was a disinterested student at best. But there was a wealth of resources out there for self-improvement and learning that I had never even considered. Much of it free.

Since then, I'd been studying relentlessly. Teaching myself programming, the basics of database development and reading up on all things digital marketing. I'd even created several micro-sites for some of our upcoming events, all designed and hand coded by myself. They were only small and nothing overly showy: a little HTML, a little CSS and a smidgen of JavaScript. All words I had never even heard of not too long ago. But they looked great (if I do say so myself) and the clients gave some really good feedback.

I'd even moved on to some of the more complex programming languages, although the options were a little overwhelming. Great names though—Python, C#, Java and, my particular favourite for obvious reasons, Ruby on Rails.

A year on, alongside the IT guy – or 'Dave' as I liked to call him – I'd somehow become the de facto digital marketing and web person in the company. Not that my salary or title reflected that workload; however, I had high hopes of that being corrected. In fact, a meeting had been called first thing Monday morning by big boss Oliver and the head of HR. I didn't see what else it could mean except a well-deserved promotion and a permanent position for yours truly. I was feeling positively giddy about the prospect.

According to Phil, it was a super-competitive profession and I needed to temper my expectations. In a way, I knew he was right, but I also didn't think he realised how much this had just clicked with me. Like suddenly I'd discovered, a little late in life to be sure, what it was I was supposed to be doing.

But I also knew nobody was going to hire me with no real experience and no relevant qualifications. That's why the meeting was so important. If I could just get the promotion. Something official. Then my foot would be well and truly wedged in the door.

Unfortunately, there was still plenty to learn, hence me blearily pretending to read the article. Eventually I admitted defeat. My concentration was no match for my excited nerves about tomorrow's meeting and the slightly disquieting anxiety I'd been feeling over how last night had played out.

We'd been out as usual with Phil's circle of school friends. People he'd known for years and the Wags, their wives and girlfriends, who all had names like Minty and Tiffy. Some of them were fairly interchangeable but Francesca, *call me Frannie*, always seemed to be around.

I suppose I got on fine with her. It was just that it always felt like there was some sort of undercurrent that I couldn't define whenever we met. Like everything she said had a sharp edge under the sugar surface. I was probably being oversensitive, because if I was truly honest, she made me feel insecure and unpolished. My accent was cockney, hers was cut glass. I went to the local comprehensive and left school at sixteen. She went to Cambridge and wasn't afraid to mention it—a lot.

Ruby, on the other hand, was more succinct about the bad vibes I got from Frannie. 'She wants to fuck your boyfriend, babes,' Ruby said.

The night before, Frannie had been on fine form, dressed super casually in that way only the super-rich can pull off. Tanned, buffed and highlighted to peroxided perfection. She hung off Phil's every last word, while her chinless wonder of a husband, Sebastian, *call me Seb,* ignored the whole situation.

He was more interested in drooling drunkenly over the eighteen-year-old barmaid. She deflected his interest with a practised ease that I recognised all too well from my own experience working behind a bar. God, men were fools sometimes.

Frannie and Seb lived in a super posh pad in Chelsea and I kind of suspected that Phil only kept up the friendship with Seb for his connections. He was a bit of a drip to be honest, despite the impressive resume. And a horrible drunk. I couldn't imagine a woman like Frannie, who had the emotional depth of a baked bean, looking at him twice if it weren't for the bank balance and the hereditary title.

I think that was why I'd had a few extra glasses of wine last night. Phil's friends and the Wags were all big drinkers anyway. Anyone who couldn't keep up was relentlessly mocked. I often felt out of place and uncomfortable around them; they tended to talk across me rather than to me, like I was some sort of temporary inconvenience they had to put up with until Phil the Magnificent came to his senses. Couple that with Frannie's incessant flirting and, long story short, my hangover was totally her fault.

Still, Phil had never given me any reason to doubt him. It wasn't his fault if that thirsty cow couldn't keep her tongue in her mouth around him. She could flirt all she liked—I was the one Phil loved, the one who shared a beautiful home with him. I was the one who, in all probability, he was going to marry one day.

Our flat *was* beautiful. Like something you'd see in a glossy magazine. I could never have believed I would live somewhere so lavish. Running my fingers along the clean white surfaces, there were moments when it felt more like a show home than somewhere a couple might actually live. It frightened me sometimes, all that sparkle, gleam, and polish. As if I wasn't good enough for my own home, which was a pretty dumb thing to think.

Ten minutes later, I was finally absorbed in a podcast, much easier than reading in my hungover state, when the front door slammed loudly. Ah shoot, Phil was back from the gym. I scampered upstairs to run a comb through my hair and stick a bra on before he saw me in all my resplendent, hungover glory.

Three

I woke up on Monday morning after a good night's sleep feeling totally revived. Excited and nervous about the day ahead, I went through my usual morning routine with extra care. I even exfoliated my elbows, not sure why. Just seemed like the thing to do.

In the bathroom I slathered myself from head to toe with the good body lotion, usually reserved for date night. While my lotion dried, I moisturised and primed my face then slapped on a coat of foundation. Whisked some blush over my cheekbones. A lick of mascara and I was done.

I padded back to the bedroom to get dressed, pulling on undies, tights, spanks and the new skirt-suit I'd bought especially for today. I did a little spin in front of the mirror. I'd spent quite a lot of money on the suit and it really was quite flattering.

'Looking good, Daisy old girl,' I said, blowing

myself a kiss. Feeling ready to take on the world, I bounced downstairs to the kitchen.

Phil, of course, was up already, looking dapper in his good blue suit. I gave him a peck on the cheek and poured myself a coffee.

'You've got your good suit on today.'

'Have I? Well you know, I always like to make an effort,' he said. *Alright, no need to be weird about it*, I thought, popping a couple of slices of bread in the toaster.

'You're back on bread then?' Phil said. Actually, I was never off it, but sometimes it was easier to just go along with Phil's health fads. He'd be on to something else in no time.

Over breakfast, Phil was sullen and quiet, clearly annoyed about something.

'What's wrong?'

'Nothing,' he replied. 'I just don't feel like talking to you right now.'

'Why?' I asked, racking my brains for something I'd done wrong. We'd had Sunday dinner yesterday with his family, but I couldn't think of anything I'd done that could have upset him. Sometimes he just got in moods for no reason.

'Please, Daisy, why do you have to always read into things? I just would like a little peace and quiet while I eat my breakfast. Not everybody needs to be constantly talking on and on.'

'What do you mean by that?' I said, stung. 'I just wanted to know what was wrong with you.'

'See,' Phil said. 'That's the problem right there. I've just told you nothing's bothering me and yet you still can't let it go. Like yesterday. You're nearly thirty years old, for Christ's sake. I'm not sure my entire family wants to listen to your fantasies of becoming, what, some famous web designer in quite such excruciating detail.'

'They asked me,' I said, wounded by the sarcasm. 'Why are you bringing this up now? You know I've got my meeting today.'

Phil sighed and shook his head. 'They were just being polite. You've got street smarts, Daisy darling, no one can deny that. It's just that you're not necessarily book smart. Let's forget about it, eh? You know I hate it when we argue. I just don't want you to be disappointed, that's all.'

I sniffed back tears. 'I know that, Phil.'

'And before you get the wrong end of the stick entirely, why don't you take a look at this?'

Leaning down by his seat, Phil lifted a flat, rectangular package onto the kitchen table with a loud, cheery 'Ta dah!'

It was beautifully gift wrapped, with a big bow on top.

'See, I'm not as bad as all that,' Phil said, radiating charm again. 'I did go to the trouble of getting you a good luck present.'

I reached out my hand but stopped just shy of touching the wrapping, as if I was waiting for it to disappear.

'Open it then,' he said. 'Oh, come on, you're not going to sulk, are you?'

I shook my head, not trusting myself to speak, and tore into the wrapping.

'Phil, it's beautiful,' I said, taking out a gorgeous leather satchel. It really was quite lovely and expensive-looking too.

'Just like a real designer would have,' he said, all proud of himself. He came around the breakfast bar and planted a kiss on my cheek. 'Love you, Goose.'

Just then my mobile phone began to vibrate. The theme tune to *Jaws* rang out across the kitchen.

'Your mother's on the phone,' Phil said wryly.

I grinned, picked it up, and opened my mouth to say hi. But Mum was already in full flow. It was how our conversations normally began and usually ended, and it had been that way ever since I was a kid. To this day, Mum never tired of telling me what to do, and what not to do, and what would happen if I didn't heed her precious advice. Maybe some of this advice wasn't so bad, but it wore me out always having to hear it. Most of these words of wisdom related to Phil nowadays. How to keep hold of him. How to get him to marry me. Nothing, to Mum's way of thinking, could be more important than that.

It still astonished her that he'd chosen to date me in the first place and that he hadn't dumped me yet. It was pretty insulting, but of course Mum didn't see it that way—she thought she was only looking out for my best interests.

In her defence, a lot of this had to do with my dad and the way in which he'd left us. You hear about these married men who nip out for a pack of cigarettes and are never seen again. In Dad's case, it was the *Evening Standard*. The next we learned of him was a postcard from Australia a fortnight later, where, as it turned out, he'd decided to make a new life for himself. It wasn't that he didn't love us – he didn't want us to think that, said the message – it was just he had this sudden thirst for pastures new. These new pastures we later discovered involved an Amazonian yoga instructor from Perth and her three cute kids.

Mum had never really recovered, which was hardly surprising, and ever afterwards she'd prized stability above all else. Little wonder she'd sought this in her second marriage, instead of romance and excitement, and wanted the same for me.

Several years after I'd left home, Mum had married Gerald Wylie, a widower from Chiswick. In my opinion, Gerald was already wedded—to his model railway set. His real pride and joy. Being his wife meant having to listen to Gerald waffle on about his lifelong hobby endlessly. But Mum seemed happy enough to comply, which was infuriating as she never bloody listened when I had something to say.

I was less interested in Gerald's infernal witterings. But if I ever tried to change the topic, his face clouded over and, with a raised eyebrow and a meaningful glance to my mother that seemed to say, 'I don't know how you put up with it all these years,' he would flounce off to play with his choo-choo trains.

Mum would stare after him admiringly as he trotted off to run the West Coast line. 'He couldn't be any less like your father.'

I knew she still beat herself up about it, falling for a charmer, a chancer, a jack the lad—all the things Dad was. None of which could be said about Gerald, the most boring man I'd ever met. Still, Mum thought I should take a leaf out of her book and show a keen interest in all of Phil's hobbies. It was this she was waffling on about now.

'If he's down the gym, you should be down there with him. It stands to reason—you don't want him mingling with any lycra-clad sexpots.'

Sexpots! Dear God, Mum. Finally, she paused to dunk a biscuit in her tea. The only time I could ever get a word in.

'Has it not occurred to you,' I answered, 'that Phil might want his own time and space?'

At this, Mum snorted down the phone. 'If you have any sense, you won't give him too much of either. You should always be there with a word of comfort, looking to soothe Phil's troubled brow.'

'For goodness' sake, Mum—I'm his girlfriend not his nursemaid!'

'I'm only saying, Daisy, you should play to your strengths.'

The unspoken suggestion here was obvious. My strengths didn't include being especially attractive or desirable. It was far from the first time Mum had implied this. As usual, I let it go. I knew she cared for me in her own way, but Lord did she have a funny way of showing it.

As Mum rabbited on, I checked my watch. I needed to leave in fifteen minutes. I went upstairs, putting her on speaker, paying little mind to what she was saying. In this way, I was able to straighten my hair and pop on some lippy without adding as much as 'yes' or 'no'.

'You look nice,' Phil said, coming into the bedroom and swatting my bum. His earlier bad mood seemed to be forgotten.

'Oh, is that Phillip?' Mum trilled. She was literally obsessed with him and flirted with my boyfriend outrageously whenever she got the chance.

He shook his head, backing rapidly away, mouthing, 'Nooooo.' The swine!

'Mum,' I said, 'I can't speak for long. I've got to get to work.'

'Still at the little temping job, Daisy?' she asked. 'Of course, once you and Phillip tie the knot, I don't suppose he'll expect you to work anymore.'

'If you must know…'

Mum talked over me. 'Remember,' she said, 'you're not getting any younger, Daisy, dear. You need to get that one tied down, start making babies. He's quite the catch.' And back we were, to that again.

'He hasn't asked me yet,' I said, through gritted teeth, as she knew perfectly well. 'Anyway Mum, I'm probably going to get a promotion soon, so there won't be time for babies for at least another ten years, maybe fifteen.'

'Daisy,' she gasped. 'Think of your ovaries. They'll never hold out that long.'

'Just kidding, Mum.'

'Of course you are, dear.'

'You know I want to have a family someday. But Phil wants to wait a few more years and I agree. There's plenty of time.'

'There is?'

'Mum, God. I'm twenty-six, not eighty-six.'

'Well,' Mum said, 'you could always force the issue. That's what I did with your father.'

I bit back a mean retort. That didn't work out too well for anyone.

'Mum, I'm not going to do that,' I said.

'The clock's ticking, that's all I'm saying.'

I rolled my eyes and finished the last section of hair. Managing to tame my unruly curls into a sleek, straight do every morning was hard work.

'Mum, I've got to go, Phil's waiting.'

'Oh well,' she said, 'in that case, bye darling.'

I hung up the phone. Took a few deep breaths. Once I got this promotion, she'd have to start taking my job a little more seriously, than thinking of it as something I did to fill in the time until Phil decided to impregnate me.

'I'm not a prize bloody heifer,' I muttered to myself.

'What's that, Goose?' Phil said from the doorway.

'Nothing, hon.'

'Well, hurry up or you're going to miss your train.' Shoot, that would be just perfect. I hurried down the stairs, grabbed my handbag and set off on foot towards the station.

Four

It was only a short distance to work, but I did worry a little about all the fumes I must have been breathing in on my daily walk. God only knew what it was doing to my lungs. The roads were gridlocked the entire way, the cars roaring out clouds of pollution. Maybe I'd get myself one of those surgeons' masks like the cyclists wore.

The lights at the pedestrian crossing opposite the train station seemed to take an age to change. Tapping my foot impatiently, I checked my watch. Five minutes until my train left. I stabbed at the button, which made not the blindest bit of difference.

Finally, thank goodness, the lights changed. I hurried across the road and into the station. Quickly swiped my Oyster card and trotted onto the escalators, holding on to the rail for dear life. I hated the damned things; they always made me feel dizzy, like I was going to topple over for no reason and roll back down to the bottom.

To distract myself I internally rehearsed my acceptance speech: *Why Oliver, I would love to work here on a permanent basis. My work is extremely impressive, do you really think so? Exemplary! Oh you're too kind.*

In reality, I was more likely to get blood out of a stone than any kind of compliment from Oliver, but whatever, that was what a fantasy life was for. Well, one of the things, anyway.

I got to the platform just as my train was pulling in. Shit. I pushed my way through packs of commuters who all seemed to lack basic spatial awareness, simple manners, or the basic tenets of personal hygiene in some cases. I jumped on just as the doors slid shut and we all did our daily dance, tussling for a seat. Bagging one, I quickly organised myself before I got too squished to move.

I pulled out my iPad, plugged in my headphones and watched a video tutorial to pass the time on the commute, trying not to brood over my earlier conversation with Phil. In the course of ten minutes, he'd shown me his worst side, quickly followed by his best, which was often the way with him. But now wasn't the time to dwell on it. Any of it. Not with the prospect of promotion looming large on the horizon. I, Daisy Monroe, was about to move up in the world!

Five

'Morning Daisy,' Laura on reception said as I pushed through the revolving doors at the front of our office block. She was pecking away at her keyboard with extremely long and impractical nails. I wondered how she ever got anything done.

'Morning,' I replied, swiping myself in.

'Nice weekend?'

'Not bad, you?'

'Oh, you know,' Laura said. 'Once you have kids, it's all nappies and breast pumps.'

At this, I nodded sagely, thinking of the wine-soaked weekend just gone.

'Oh sorry,' Laura said, looking as though she'd just remembered I had a terminal disease. 'You don't have children yet, do you, Daisy?'

'Nope,' I said, eyeing the elevator. The glowing numbers showed it was still on the top floor and not moving. 'Plenty of time for all that,' I said, backing away. Why was everyone so obsessed with the contents of my womb? Laura nodded sympathetically. A comic-book style speech-bubble saying, 'Tick Tock,' was practically floating above her head.

I decided not to wait for the lift. It was only two flights, and if I took the stairs, I could feel virtuous about getting some more of my daily steps in while avoiding any further well-intentioned negging from Laura.

I arrived in the office, huffing a little. I was one of the first in as usual. Dave the IT guy waved at me across the office floor.

'Everything okay?' I asked.

'Yup. No issues.'

'That's how I like it.'

'I've got some server patches scheduled for later in the day,' he said, 'shouldn't be any downtime.'

'Don't forget to take a backup this time,' I said. I didn't want a repeat of the fiasco a few months back, when the website had been down for an hour and we'd had to restore it from an old version, losing weeks of work. We'd both gotten the bollocking of our lives for that one.

'Daisy, mate,' Dave said, 'you need to let that go.'

'Never,' I said overdramatically. I really liked Dave. In general, people in the office seemed to find his blunt style off-putting. But he meant well, and he could have been a lot more obstructive, having been lumbered with a panicking noob like me. Instead, he seemed to relish having someone who was actually interested in learning. To be fair, he did go on a bit, but that was just Dave.

I popped my coat on the hook and surveyed the rest of the office. At some point the sales team – three overconfident members of Gen Z who never reached the office before nine and seemed perpetually hungover – would start to drift in. The head of HR and the business development director each had their own office and a PA. Pam, the office manager, had her own desk in the open plan part of the office.

My desk faced Oliver's PA, a brittle fifty-something named Amelia who'd been with the company for donkey's years, and whose lackey I was initially supposed to be. Since I'd taken on my extra duties, she'd become extremely snooty about my "*elevation*" as she called it.

We were both parked outside Oliver's office so he could bark orders at us and holler at me to fetch him coffee from the comfort of his own desk. Amelia should have been thankful it was now me he was yelling at, instead of her.

Oliver wasn't here yet, so that gave me a little time to settle in and start working through the few emails that had come in over the weekend. Our meeting was scheduled for ten and I could feel the anticipation settling like a ball of yarn in the pit of my stomach.

Amelia bustled in. 'Morning Daisy,' she said, looking faintly disapproving.

'Morning,' I answered guardedly; then we made awkward small talk while her computer booted up.

'I see you're having a meeting with Oliver at ten,' she said. Checking his schedule was the first thing she did each day, even before checking her emails.

'That's right,' I replied.

She gave me an odd little smile.

'Well, I'm sure it's nothing to worry about.'

The bitch was trying to psych me out and not for the first time.

'I'm not worried,' I said. God, why did she have to be so thoroughly unpleasant? I saw Amelia suddenly snap to attention. She started furiously typing. Oliver must have arrived. If he ever spotted you with nothing to do, he made a point of lumbering you with some shitty menial task just to make a point. I followed Amelia's lead and pretended to check my voice mail.

'Morning ladies,' Oliver said, sweeping past in a cloud of expensive cologne and stale cigarettes. 'Amelia, be a love and bring me a coffee.'

She shot daggers at me. Okay, this was new. Hopefully, it was a good sign.

The next hour crawled by. Finally, the hands on the big wall clock slotted into position. It was ten o'clock.

I took a deep breath – *Come on Daisy, girl.* I pushed my chair back from my desk and nervously straightened my skirt, smoothing it down so it sat flattened against my thighs. I took another deep breath and then, ignoring Amelia, poked my head into Oliver's office.

Oliver was behind his desk, deep in conversation with Judith, the HR director, who was sitting in the chair next to him. I rapped on the door and they both fell silent.

'Ah, Daisy here you are,' he said after a beat. 'Please sit.'

I slid into a chair opposite them and put on my most confident smile, which admittedly faltered somewhat when neither of them returned it.

'So…' Oliver said, sharing a glance with Judith that I couldn't quite interpret. My stomach fluttered. The mood in the room felt tense.

He cleared his throat. 'Thank you for joining us this morning.'

Oliver saying thank you. Damn, something was definitely up.

'You should know that we've been extremely pleased with your work over the last year, Daisy,' he continued.

I let out a whoosh of air that I wasn't even aware I'd been holding and settled back into my chair. This was more like it.

Oliver droned on as if unaware that the suspense

was killing me. I smiled encouragingly, thinking, *Spit it out, you old windbag.*

'It's really brought home the need for us as a company to be more digitally focused. And that's why we've decided to hire a full-time digital marketing manager.'

Oh wow. It was really happening!

'Unfortunately, and you must believe me when I say that this is not a decision we've taken lightly by any means, have we, Judith?'

Judith shook her head, looking distinctly uncomfortable. Wait what, unfortunately? That didn't sound good. I suddenly realised I'd lost track of what Oliver was saying. I refocused.

'Unfortunately,' there was that word again, 'this means that your admin role is no longer available.'

Oh God, was he saying what I thought he was saying?

'And the manager role?' I heard myself say over the pounding in my ears.

Oliver paused then nodded. 'We've decided the new role should be filled by someone with a little more…experience.'

'Oh,' I said as no other response sprang to mind.

'Oliver's brother-in-law has a degree in marketing,' Judith piped up. She was one of those people who always felt the need to fill an uncomfortable silence. 'We're lucky to get him, actually.'

Oliver shot her an impatient look. He definitely hadn't wanted me to have that information, seemed like the game had been rigged the whole time. As usual, I was the last one to know.

'Daisy,' he said, 'I'm afraid this means we're letting you go.'

'But you just said I've been doing a good job,' I whispered.

'Well, surely you didn't expect…' Oliver ran out of words and looked askance at Judith.

He couldn't be so oblivious to other people's feelings as to think I wouldn't be blindsided by this. No, he knew all right. He was just trying to shift the blame, make it look like I was the one being unreasonable. The coward.

My face went bright red, my eyes welling up with tears. This was not how I saw the day panning out. Oliver sighed. Growing impatient with the whole ordeal, he dropped any pretence of empathy like it was hot.

'Now then, Daisy, this was always meant to be a temporary position. You knew that from the start. I would say you've done rather better out of it than you first expected.'

I opened my mouth, but Oliver didn't give me a chance to speak. 'Judith, would you like to wrap this up?' he said, taking advantage of my inability to form a coherent sentence. Wrap this up! The bastard.

'Certainly. Daisy, as you have been here a little under two years and are on a temporary contract, we are not legally obliged to make any redundancy payments.' Oh God, I hadn't even thought of that. 'However, as a goodwill gesture,' she said, not looking me in the eye, 'we're pleased to offer you one month's pay in lieu of notice.'

'Starting from when?' I asked, my head spinning.

'Well,' Judith said, looking a little put out, 'from now, I'm afraid.'

Six

The train journey home passed in a blur. To be treated like that after I had half killed myself for them over the last year. To be humiliated and escorted out of the building like some kind of criminal, tracked by Amelia's smirking face.

I would have to tell everyone. Mum, Phil, Phil's family. Oh God, I thought about Frannie patronisingly patting my knee in the pub over the weekend. 'Good for you,' she'd said when I told her about my, it turned out, imaginary promotion. My face burned with embarrassment.

I hadn't realised until this point just how high I had built my hopes up. I wondered how long they'd been stringing me along for. It had been foolish of me to imagine I'd ever be hired for such a job. Of course, I could try to find something else, but no one in their right mind was going to hand me the kind of role I'd set my heart on. All anyone would see on my CV was that I'd been temping. I wouldn't even get through the front door. A tear trickled down my cheek. I swiped it away, determined not to start crying on the tube.

I tried to phone Phil, desperate to hear a friendly voice. His phone rang a few times and then went through to his voice mail. I hung up without leaving a message and spent the rest of the journey staring out of the window, trying not to dissolve into tears.

The rocking motion of the train felt strangely soothing and by the time I got to my station I felt a lot calmer, although numb might be a better way of putting it. Suddenly I wasn't sure I wanted to speak to Phil at all. I knew that he'd want to help, but I also knew what he'd really be thinking: *I told you so, silly Goose.*

As I rounded the corner onto our street, I saw Phil's car in the driveway. My heart lifted. He was home early for some reason. All of a sudden, I desperately wanted to see him. Didn't matter if he said the wrong thing. All I wanted was someone on my side, someone who loved me, someone to wrap me in a bear hug and tell me that everything was going to be okay. And if he also threatened to key Oliver's car, well, I was all right with that too.

At the front door, I fumbled in my oversized handbag. My keys made a bid for freedom, but I finally got a grip on them, pulled them out and unlocked the door.

I stepped into the hallway, ready to call out Phil's name – I didn't want to give him a fright – when I heard his voice rumbling up the hall. *Damn, he must be on the phone.* Then my chest froze. I could hear a woman's voice too. They were laughing.

Oh God, I'd have recognised that braying laugh anywhere. What was Frannie doing here? Then my stomach dropped into my stilettos because I had a pretty good idea. More rustling and giggling from down the hall. I clapped my hand over my mouth as my mind finally caught up with what my eyes were seeing.

They were at the foot of the stairs. Frannie had a foot up on my new coffee table, two arms around Phil's waist, and her tongue down my boyfriend's throat. Neither of them had noticed me yet. My brain involuntarily zoomed in on the situation. Now Frannie's hand was down the front of Phil's good blue suit. The one he must have put on this morning, especially for her. She started to unbutton it in a frenzy, tugging at his belt with her other hand.

I took a step down the hallway on legs that felt like stilts. This couldn't be happening. Only it was. My legs buckled and I slumped against the wall with a distinct thud. That got their attention all right.

'Daisy!' Phil said, his eyes wide with shock. He

pushed Frannie away and she stumbled back, hurriedly rearranging her clothing. Then she turned and fled to the sitting room. My sitting room. 'Daisy, what are you doing home?'

A hot flush bloomed prickling heat across my body. My throat felt like it was closing up. I took a step back. I couldn't breathe. I had to get out of the house. Away from them.

'Daisy, just wait.' But I couldn't. The world had descended into a red mist. All I could see was Frannie, her back arched, Phil's hands around her waist, dry humping her hand like a randy teenager. I needed to put as much distance as possible between this ugly spectacle and me.

I found myself with my handbag slung over my shoulder, halfway down our front path, with no memory of getting there.

'Daisy, wait, you're being ridiculous.'

I spun around. 'How could you?' I tried to say, but my mouth refused to cooperate, flapping uselessly.

'I'm sorry, Daisy. Babe, please, I'm so sorry, just come back in the house. Let's talk about this.'

As if I could go back inside with Frannie still holed up in there. I backed up the path, glowering at Phil, who was still standing on the doorstep, his shirt untucked, his hair awry.

'Goose, come back inside, you're making a show.'

At last, the spell seemed to break and I crashed

through the gate, stumbling out onto the street. I glanced back once. Frannie's face appeared behind Phil's shoulder. Both stared back at me as if I was the intruder.

'For Christ's sake, just let her go,' Frannie said.

I walked to the end of our street in a daze. At the corner, I looked back briefly. Phil and Frannie were now in a heated exchange on the doorstep. They appeared to have forgotten about me. She was waving her arms furiously. He seemed to be angry as hell.

I turned the corner in total shock. That was when my fight-or-flight instinct kicked in. I chose flight. I turned another corner. Then another.

Seven

My feet moved blindly, stilettos clacking on the gum-spotted pavement of the high street. It was busy, people chattering as they walked along, cars beeping in either direction. A jackhammer drill thudded close by, adding to the cacophony. There was no way I could think straight.

The sun suddenly slipped behind a cloud and I shivered. Even though it was hot, my hands felt like ice. Dizzy, I sank down onto a nearby bench. Just as well it was there; otherwise I would have fallen on my bottom. In which case, I think I would have just curled up into a ball on the pavement. This was London, so everyone would just step over me and carry on with their day.

In one fell swoop, I had no job, no boyfriend, and no home. The flat was in Phil's name, bought and paid for. I had no lasting claim on it. For the first time in years I wanted my mum. Terror welled up inside me, blocking off all rational thought. I couldn't go back, that much was clear. But I didn't have anywhere else to go.

It wasn't that I didn't have friends. Other than Ruby, I mean. I did. Looking back, though, I hadn't realised until now that Phil could be quite controlling in terms of my friendships outside his circle. There was never any yelling as such, but I was worn down by the constant low-level complaints when Phil took a dislike to someone, which was often. At the time I would have called you a liar if you'd suggested that letting those friendships drift wasn't my own decision. But it was starting to dawn on me that I may have been deluding myself about lots of things.

How many acquaintances had I let slip over the years to avoid a scene? I realised how isolated I'd become as a result. With Ruby away, there was certainly no one I could think of to turn to right now.

I put my head in my hands. No one stopped to help or ask if I was okay, which was probably a blessing. One kind word and I'd be done. A bawling mess, howling on the high street.

Inside my handbag my phone began to vibrate. I removed it with ice-cold hands. It was Phil, but there was no way I could talk to him. I doubted I could utter a single word at that moment. Finally, it stopped ringing. A moment later, a new message notification popped up. I listened to it numbly. It was Phil begging me to come home. In the background, I could hear Frannie. She was still there.

I dropped the phone like it had morphed into a venomous spider. It landed in my handbag and I zipped the bag shut, shuddering at the image.

Above me, the sky went a shade darker. An ominous rumble came from somewhere in the distance. *Oh great, just to really top off my day, it's going to start raining.* I'd barely completed the thought when the heavens did in fact open, slinging down sheets of sooty rain. My hair turned instantly into a straggling mess that would dry in bouffant curls. Not that I cared.

I looked around for somewhere to shelter. Without realising it, my feet had taken me on a familiar route. I was back, once again, at the train station. Where I'd started out, what felt like a century ago, at the beginning of this awful, never-ending, groundhog day of nightmare proportions.

I dashed across the road and into the station. Shaking off the rain, I wondered what to do next. My phone vibrated again. I didn't let it go to voicemail this time. Instead I hesitated for a moment and then switched it off.

I walked towards the ticket barriers in a daze, swiped my Oyster card and got on the first train I saw. I just needed to sit for a while. Somewhere out of the rain, where no one would pay me any attention. Where better to be ignored than the London Underground? The unwritten rule: no eye contact, no unsolicited conversation—except for to-bloody-day of course.

Several stops in, a rowdy group of men rolled onto the train. They wore assorted costumes and were swigging from large cans of beer. For reasons best known to himself, one of them was wearing a naughty nurse outfit and aggressively waving around a pair of pink fluffy handcuffs. Oh Christ, now they were singing. The doors slid shut. It was too late for me to get off. Who the hell were these people? It was Monday afternoon for heaven's sake.

'All right, darling?' the burly nurse said, planting himself next to me. I couldn't deal with this right now. I squeezed my eyes shut, hoping he'd get the message and go away. Nope. I gripped the seat and ignored him as best I could.

'Smile, love,' he said, breathing beer and garlic fumes into my face. 'It might never happen.'

I made a strange hiccupping sound, and it gave me a certain amount of perverse gratification when, like some sort of stop-motion puppet, his expression slipped from leering to confused to uncomfortable shock. *Serves you right, arsehole*, I had time to think venomously before I let out a loud, guttural wail.

The train was suddenly silent. In slow motion,

everyone turned to look at me. One of the men said, 'Darren, what did you do?'

Now I was full-on weeping, tears, snot and mascara sliding down my face. Darren tried to apologise, which set me off on another crying jag. Maybe I was laughing hysterically at the same time. It was very hard to tell.

A tense thirty seconds later, the train pulled into the next station. I stumbled onto an unfamiliar platform. As the doors slid shut, I heard a burst of laughter coming from the train behind me.

I was blinded by tears, red with embarrassment. This was a nightmare. Mortifying. People were staring at me with open concern, as if one of them might actually come over and ask me if I was okay. Unacceptable!

I fled up a flight of stairs, across an enclosed bridge that led to an open-air platform. A train sat idling. I darted through the doors just as they began to slide shut.

Relieved to see that the carriage was empty, I collapsed into a seat. Wiping my nose on the sleeve of my new shirt, I stared off into space, trying to get my breathing under control. The train pulled out of the station. I had no idea where it was going. Nor did I care.

I pressed my face against the window and watched concrete and tower blocks streaming by. The train seemed to be travelling along some sort of cross country line. It didn't seem to be stopping anywhere. Another station whizzed by. I felt a tinge of anxiety as concrete turned to suburbs and then fields and rolling hills dotted with fluffy sheep.

I shut my eyes, just for a moment. Leaning my forehead against the glass, exhaustion overwhelmed me and I fell into a deep, dreamless sleep.

'Excuse me, miss.' Someone touched me lightly on the arm. I came to with a snort. A man in a train manager's uniform apologised. 'You have to wake up,' he said, 'this is the end of the line.'

Oh shit. I sat up blearily, rubbing my eyes.

'Where are we?'

'Upper Finlay.'

'Huh?'

'Are you okay?'

I forced my face into a semblance of a smile.

'Peachy,' I said and stumbled off the train.

Eight

'You've really outdone yourself this time, Daisy,' I muttered to myself. I must have looked a right state. As predicted, my hair had gone into a riot of wild curls, and I still had on my stupid skirt suit. Somewhere along the line, just to add insult to injury, I'd also managed to ladder my tights beyond repair. My legs looked like two snakes trying to shed their skins. Luckily, by this stage I was way past caring.

That said, I was a little ashamed of myself. The last few hours were a blank, punctuated by mortifying incidents. I would have expected to deal with something like this calmly, rationally. Not like some hysterical, out-of-control maniac.

I winced, remembering my breakdown on the train. I think I might have been in some kind of fugue state. Like one of those people you read about in trashy thrillers who murders someone and then doesn't remember doing it.

At least I didn't have any more tears left in my body to cry. I was practically a desiccated husk. One strong puff of wind and I'd crumble to dust and blow away.

I squinted up at the minuscule print of the train timetable pinned to the information board, trying to make sense of the incomprehensible letters and numbers and randomly colour-coded lines. I needed to get myself back to London, book into a cheap hotel, sink a few glasses of wine and sleep. I'd worry about tomorrow, tomorrow.

Ah, balls. The next train wasn't for another four hours. And even then, it looked as though I'd have to change several times. Where the actual hell was I?

I looked around, taking in my surroundings properly for the first time. The station was tiny and on any other day I would have thought it quite pretty, with a cute little waiting room (closed of course), a covered bench and hanging baskets full of pink and yellow flowers. The air smelt of honeysuckle and some subtle citrus flavour I couldn't identify, Eau de Not Pollution maybe.

A bee spiralled past my nose, buzzing cheerfully. I could hear birds singing but also very faintly the hum of passing cars. I hadn't eaten anything since picking at my breakfast that morning and I was suddenly ravenous. And really, really thirsty.

I had several hours to kill; maybe it was worth exploring a little. I crunched across the gravel towards a white picket fence. A blue-and-white painted sign said, 'Finlay village ¼ mile.' Okay, that looked promising. I decided to check it out.

I crossed a small car park and wandered down a gravel path, which opened out onto a tree-lined country road. *Right then, let's see where this takes me.*

I started walking, carefully navigating the uneven pavement and admiring the large ivy-covered houses, set back on neatly tended lawns that lined the right hand side of the road. Across from me, a pretty canal flowed past; beyond that, nothing but green, rolling hills.

Just as I was starting to worry I might be lost, another sign for the village appeared. I checked my watch. I still had plenty of time until the next train departed. The thought of heading back to London gave me a little depressed dip. Being here was sort of an adventure, taking my mind off the real world while I explored this one instead.

I passed an old stone church, its grounds dotted with tombstones. Here and there the road branched off into hiking trails, at the head of which small groups of men and women in bright jackets and hiking boots congregated. A car whizzed past. I was getting nearer to civilisation.

I rounded a bend. Finally, a street with shops on

it. For the first time that day, I felt my spirits lift. I hadn't gotten myself into some sort of *Deliverance*-style mess; this was a perfectly nice little village.

Cute stone cottages lined the road, with neat squares of lawn out front and brightly painted doors. A profusion of small cobbled alleys ran off the main road. This was the sort of place you might want to explore on a day trip. I didn't feel like exploring now, especially not in these damned shoes. But I felt confident that I could at least waste a couple of hours here.

I spied a pub at the midpoint of the street. Bingo! A couple of stiff G and T's would be just the ticket. Further up the street I could see a row of shops and even an old-fashioned red post box.

On closer inspection, the pub looked a bit intimidating. A group of men in high-vis jackets sat on the benches outside, smoking and laughing uproariously. I didn't know if I wanted to go in there on my own.

My initial boost of confidence had been short-lived. Maybe I could just go back to the platform and wait there. My stomach rumbled. I was tired and thirsty, and my feet throbbed painfully. Sod it, I was going in.

I could feel several sets of eyes on me as I approached the pub, my shoes ringing out against the cobbles. It was enough to set me on edge and I quickened my pace. Chickening out at the last moment, I hurried past the huddle of workmen.

The whole idea of going for a wander in the middle of nowhere suddenly seemed a lot less appealing. I didn't even know where I was. And nor did anyone else for that matter. Not Phil, not my mum. I'd dropped off the map, or as good as. Maybe not the best plan. And yet I left my phone switched off, summoning what little defiance I could muster.

I turned one last corner, on the verge of heading back, and that was when I saw it. Some fifty yards ahead of me was a small café with a few tables and chairs arranged out front. I breathed a sigh of relief and headed towards it fingers and toes, figuratively, crossed.

The shop front was faded and a little weather-worn, but it had a welcoming air that spurred me onwards and put a little spring back in my step.

Crossing the back alley, my happy suspicions were confirmed. The gnarled wooden bench out front sported an empty coffee cup and the sign set out on the pavement advertised tea and fresh sandwiches. My stomach growled at the thought of thick sliced bread (who cared what was in it) and a much needed hot brew.

A towering stack of books leaned precariously by the entrance. On the wall above the front door, a peeling green-and-gold sign read 'The Bookshop

Café.' As I took hold of the brass door handle, the musty smell of old books wafted up. I breathed in the comforting familiar aroma.

The smell was nostalgic, reminding me of my childhood. As a kid I'd always had my nose buried in a book, spending many happy hours holed up at the local library. It was long gone now, of course. Another victim of crippling budget cuts. But my love of reading had never gone away. Not that I'd had much time for it lately, what with the job and the mammoth workload. Welp, that wasn't a problem any longer. Thanks to shitty Oliver. Maybe it was time to work my way through the classics. I could actually read all those books I'd fibbed about reading in the past.

This place was a godsend. It looked safe enough, and I could kill two birds with one stone; line my stomach with a stodgy snack and select a comfort read for the journey back to London. I could lose myself in a novel; immerse myself in someone else's desperate adventures. After everything that had happened today, I'd had enough adventure of my own to last me a lifetime.

I pushed open the door. The little bell above it rang merrily, announcing my presence. Taking a deep breath, I stepped out of the bright sunlight and into the dim, cosy interior of the Bookshop Café.

Nine

'Wow,' I said, my mouth forming a little round O of delight. I had stepped into an old-fashioned bookshop, filled with rows and rows of shelves, tightly packed with books of all descriptions. Rolling ladders clung to dizzyingly tall units. Above me, a gallery with a rail was lined with yet more books. Inside the shop, the heady aroma of old pages grew even more intense.

The hardwood floor was a little scuffed but dotted with comfy looking armchairs. The room was lit by pretty antique lamps, so the space felt cosy instead of intimidating. A few motes of golden dust spun around in the sleepy air. Although the place had seen better days, it still retained oodles of authentic charm that any hipster outlet would have died for. The atmosphere was calm and comforting. It was a place to dream the afternoons away.

Everywhere I looked, some little treasure awaited

me. A beautiful oil painting, shining deep purples and browns, an old-fashioned typewriter on an antique desk, a stone fireplace, sooty with use.

Peering into the recesses of the shop I could see a maze of rooms and corridors leading off in seemingly random directions. The Bookshop Café appeared to be some kind of TARDIS. Bigger on the inside than out. No café in sight though. My stomach rumbled again. I felt like I might eat one of the books if I couldn't get my hands on a biscuit and a cup of tea.

I appeared to be the only customer on the premises and the long, wooden counter by the window was empty. Seriously starved, I pressed on further into the shop. The feeling of opportunity and adventure that I had felt earlier began to rise in me again, even more so when I drifted under an arch and paused for a while in the children's section. I slid out a copy of *Swallows and Amazons* and held it to my nose, breathing the scent in deeply. Childhood memories of adventure and escapism swirled through my mind.

I thought I spotted a sign for the café and chased it—Alice down the rabbit hole. Boxes and boxes of books lined the walkways. I poked my head into a small cubbyhole. A secret room lined with more books.

I drifted on, totally entranced, past brightly coloured graphic novels and into the classics section. I ran my hand along the row of titles, stopping at a lovely hardbound copy of *Pride and Prejudice*. I traced a finger over its embossed cover, about to open it up, when I heard a loud commotion behind me; the scrabbling sound of nails sliding across the hardwood floor.

'Wolf!' a male voice exclaimed sharply. 'Stop!'

'Huh?'

I spun around then froze on the spot as I saw what was heading my way; a large dog bounded, splay-legged, across the shop floor towards me. A Great Dane. Its eyes were rolling comically, its tail wagging furiously. Behind the dog, a man clattered down a spiral staircase that seemed to have appeared out of nowhere.

I had just enough time to register the impression of casual, well-fitted clothes – jeans and a T-shirt – because Wolf clearly had no intention of stopping. If anything, the dog sped up, grinning wildly.

'Wolf, you devil, stop! Do as you're told for once!'

The dog picked up its pace, wearing a goofy grin, delighting in its disobedience. I looked towards the voice. A man stood at the foot of the staircase. He was around my age, tall, with broad shoulders and tousled brown hair. Deep, dark, Darcy-Firth eyes regarded me from behind black-rimmed glasses.

Something like a shock went through me when our eyes connected. Flustered, I took a step back to make some room between us. Big mistake.

I had forgotten about the dog, who was now winding himself around my legs excitedly. Wolf gave an apologetic bark as I began to topple, slapstick style, over his back.

'Oh bloody hell,' the man said, starting forward to catch me. But he was much too late. I fell backwards in slow-mo, the copy of *Pride and Prejudice* flying from my hand.

Wolf gave a yelp and shot off with his tail between his legs. I flailed with my hands, toppling a display of tourist leaflets on the way down. My stupid, dumb stilettos came out from under me and I landed on my bottom with a *whumf*, legs akimbo.

Above me, a hardback copy of Edgar Allen Poe's *Collected Works* teetered on the edge of the topmost shelf and then plummeted, conking me on the back of my head. Somewhere I thought I heard a raven squawk.

I looked at the chaos scattered all around me and put my hand on the back of my skull.

The Great Dane had rejoined its owner. Master wasn't the right word, obviously. Wolf was clearly his own boss. In fairness to the big dog, the grin had disappeared, replaced by a soulful stare. He appeared to be saying, *I'm sorry. You know how it is. Sometimes you just need to cut loose.*

'Wolf, now you've gone and done it,' said the man, who – now that my wits were a bit more collected – I noticed was rather handsome. He sounded more worried than angry. Wolf whined and made a tactical retreat.

Reaching down, the man unceremoniously hauled me to my feet. I dusted myself off and gave him my full attention. He regarded me with a look of concern.

More than a little flustered, I took another step backwards. This time a box of books clipped my heels. *Oh, come on!* I thought as I started to lose my balance for a second time. The man lurched forward and grabbed my arm, saving me at the last moment. We both stared down at his hand as it clutched my forearm just above the wrist. He let go and held up his hands.

'Thanks,' I said, going a fetching shade of red. Blushing on top of everything. *Way to go, Daisy.*

He shot me an awkward look. 'Do you think you could show your gratitude by not suing me? That would be an enormous help.'

'It's all right,' I said. 'Honestly, I'm fine. These things happen.'

Despite the threat of a lawsuit lifting, the man still appeared worried. His dark eyes scanned my face closely. I must have looked an absolute mess.

'You don't look fine,' he said, 'if you don't mind me saying.'

I wanted to deny it. I really did. But his show

of sympathy crumbled my last remaining shred of composure, and thinking, *Oh no Daisy, you wet rag, not again*, I promptly burst into tears.

'I'm so sorry,' he said, looking mortified.

'It's not you,' I said through hiccups. 'Everything went wrong long before all this.'

'Well, whoever's to blame, I think you'd better sit down while I make you a pot of tea.'

I perked up a little. 'And maybe a couple of biscuits?'

The man treated me to a dazzling smile. A brilliant ray of sunshine. A ridiculously cute dimple appeared on his left cheek.

'I think we can go one better than that. How do you feel about cake?'

'Very positively indeed,' I said.

Ten

After gently guiding me towards the nearest armchair, my host disappeared down one of the narrow corridors. I sank into corduroy cushions and let the comfy seat take my whole sorry weight. *Well, this is embarrassing*, I thought, reduced to snuffling now but feeling a little better than I had a few minutes earlier.

It was hard to believe you could fit so much shame and misery into a single day. I felt my head again, wincing. There was a nasty bump forming and a dull, throbbing pain to go with it.

The man reappeared before I could dwell on my sorrows for too long. He was carrying a large wooden tray, laden with goodies: china teapot, ceramic cup, jug of milk, and a whopping great slice of chocolate cake.

'Here you go,' he said, bending down and placing the tray next to me on a side table.

'Thanks,' I said. 'That looks great. Just what the doctor ordered.'

Straightening up, he reached his hand towards the back of my head but stopped short of touching it.

'Do you mind if I just take a quick look?'

I shook my head, signalling permission, and he gently pushed back my hair.

Oh boy, he smelt like cedar. I tried not to sniff him. *Rein it in, Daisy.* Jeez, maybe the bump on my head was worse than I thought.

'No permanent damage done,' he said, sitting in the armchair opposite me and staring deep into my eyes. Inexplicably, my heart started to beat a little faster. Well, maybe it wasn't *so* inexplicable. I might have been slightly traumatised, but I wasn't blind.

I pushed my hair away from my face. Not in a girlish, flirty way. More like a stroppy teenager. I wiped my nose on my sleeve. *If you think I'm in any mood to be flirting with handsome strangers, you've got another think coming*, I thought.

Then I felt instantly guilty. Sure, his dog had knocked me on my bum, but he had been extremely apologetic. The man that is. The dog couldn't have cared less. With no sense of shame about all the trouble he'd caused, Wolf had plonked himself on top of my feet and promptly gone to sleep, his tail thumping rhythmically.

Anyway, the man can't help being good-looking, I

thought begrudgingly. A lock of hair fell over his eyes and he pushed his glasses up onto his forehead, sweeping his hair away from his face.

'They're just for reading,' he said, regarding me with a hint of a smile. Then he shrugged. 'Which is pretty much compulsory in this job.'

Part of me wanted to be distracted by a little flirtation with a good-looking man, but mostly I felt bone-weary. A touch delirious even. And stupidly, like doing so would be some kind of betrayal to Phil, I sank further into the armchair. God, I was a fool.

'Does your head hurt?' he asked. 'Maybe I can get you something for it.'

I shook my head. The pain seemed to have magically died down. Apparently, covertly sniffing a handsome man was an effective painkiller. Who knew!

He regarded me with a wary frown, worried, I expect, that I might burst into another round of hysterical weeping.

'So,' I said after an awkward pause, 'here you are delivering first aid, and I don't even know your name.'

'Alex,' he answered, offering a sheepish wave. 'Alex Dean. Hi. Welcome to the Bookshop Café.'

'And what a welcome it was…'

Another look of regret crossed his face. 'I really

am sorry about Wolf's ambush. I hate to think we've added to your misery. Normally, we do a pretty good job of brightening our customers' days.'

'Well, you did brighten mine, at least to start with. What a fabulous place.' I looked around admiringly at the Aladdin's cave of books.

'Thanks. We do our best. But it's always good to hear. And what about you? I didn't catch your name…'

'It's Daisy,' I said.

'Daisy,' he repeated, as if he liked the sound of it. This struck me as a good thing as I liked the sound of him saying it.

Unable to restrain myself any longer, I picked up a dainty silver fork and broke off a massive chunk of the delicious-looking cake. Boy, did I deserve it!

Without further ado I shovelled it into my mouth. At once my taste buds started letting off fireworks and doing somersaults. I screwed up my eyes and let out a rather embarrassing moan of delight.

The corner of Alex's mouth twitched upwards. 'You like it then?'

'Oh my God, that's incredible!'

'Thanks,' he said. 'I made it myself.'

'You did not.'

Alex nodded. 'Did too. You're looking at the Bookshop Café's pastry chef.'

'Not just a pretty face then…' *Really, Daisy?*

Where did that little nugget come from? Alex treated me to another dazzling smile. Out came the dimple.

Revived by the smell of food, Wolf started to nuzzle against my legs. Alex shook his head in mock disgust. 'No cake for you, boy.'

Wolf whined, looking sorry for himself.

'Can dogs eat chocolate?' I asked. I was pretty sure it was poisonous to them. 'Nope,' Alex said, grinning. 'But he doesn't know that.'

Less immune to Wolf's charms, I ruffled the short fur above his eyes. 'Poor Wolf,' I said. 'No hard feelings. You just wanted to roll out the red carpet, didn't you, and say a great big hello.'

'Not sure you're sending out the right signal there.'

'Come on,' I said. 'I bet you spoil him something rotten.'

Alex held his hands up, admitting as much. 'You've got me. Guilty as charged. I've created a monster.'

Tutting, I stroked the top of Wolf's head. 'Have you heard what he's calling you, Wolf? A monster. That's not right, is it, boy?' Wolf rolled his eyes in full agreement, his tail thumping double time against the floor.

For the last few minutes, I'd forgotten my troubles. Only now did they return to me. On entering the bookshop, I'd guessed it was the kind of place where you could lose yourself easily. But however much I wanted to do just that, it was time to square up to reality again. I had a train back to London to catch.

'So,' Alex said, as if he'd guessed what I was thinking. 'You don't look like you're from around here.'

I gave a watery laugh. 'I don't even know where *here* is,' I admitted.

'For the record, deepest, darkest Derbyshire. But how can that be? You must have some idea of where you've got to.'

'Nope. Not really. To be honest, the whole day's been a bit of a blur.'

'Are you in some sort of trouble?' He pushed his glasses back onto his nose and peered at me through them, as though they could somehow help him figure me out. *Good luck with that,* I thought. I found myself tearing up again. My bottom lip started to wobble.

'Hey,' Alex said. 'It's okay, whatever it is, you can tell me. I don't get beautiful, mysterious strangers turning up on my doorstep just every day.'

Beautiful! I wiped my nose with my sleeve. Alex did that cute half-smile again and I thought he was probably just being kind, not taking the piss.

'Honestly,' he said. 'This is the most exciting thing that's happened to me all week.'

'I wouldn't know where to start,' I said.

'At the beginning?'

I laughed bleakly at the scale of the challenge. 'We'd be here all night in that case.'

Alex shrugged. 'I don't have anywhere else to be.'

'Speaking of which, what time is it?' I asked, deftly changing the subject. 'I have a train back to London I need to catch.'

Alex nodded at a clock on the wall. Oh no, it was six already! Alarmed by the late hour, I jumped up from my seat in a panic.

'London, you say?'

I nodded.

'That's a hell of a trek.'

It was hard to disagree. But worse than the length of the journey was the terrible uncertainty awaiting me at the end of it.

'Are there any hotels around here?' I asked. 'Preferably one star or no star. Something easy on the pocket.'

That seemed like the best bet, at least for one night. I needed to buy myself a little breathing space.

Alex shook his head. 'Not in Upper Finlay. You'd have to go another dozen miles to find anything that remotely resembled a budget option. Even then, I wouldn't say The Carlyle was all that cheap.'

I hemmed and hawed, trying to think on my feet, racked with terrible indecision.

To be honest, I had been feeling so comfortable with Alex I'd almost forgotten the reason I was here.

I suddenly felt the day crashing back down on me like a lead weight.

'Well, I can't stay here forever,' I said, looking around the homely bookshop.

'Maybe that's not such a crazy idea,' Alex said. He rubbed his hand over a jaw that was raspy with stubble.

I looked at him in astonishment. Laughing, I said, 'You think I should stay here forever?'

'Bit soon?' Alex said.

'Um...'

'Listen,' Alex said, 'I can take you to the train station, but Daisy...' My name came out gravelly, deep. It was the second time he'd said my name and I liked it just as much as I had the first time.

'You *could* stay here if you wanted.'

Oh boy, was this going to be some sort of *Indecent Proposal* type situation? *I'm listening*, my ovaries said.

'Just for tonight I mean,' Alex said, a half-smile crinkling the corners of his eyes. 'There's a room upstairs that you're welcome to use. It's a bit scruffy around the edges, but it's clean and comfortable enough.'

Sinking into bed and being done with this horrible day sounded wonderful. But of course, he was a total stranger. Alex must have caught my expression.

'It locks from the inside,' he said, deadpan.

'Oh no,' I said, 'it's not that.' Although *that* was

exactly what it was. 'It's just that I wouldn't want to be a bother.'

'No bother at all. It's not too often I get to help out a damsel in distress.'

I lifted an eyebrow.

'Too much?' Alex said.

Now I was the one smiling. I could hardly have felt more vulnerable, and I didn't know Alex from Adam, yet somehow I was completely relaxed. I decided to trust my instincts and give him the benefit of the doubt.

'Are you absolutely sure? It really isn't too much trouble?'

Alex waved the suggestion away. 'Not at all. It's only going to waste. I've been looking to rent out the flat for a while now. It's just sitting empty.'

'In that case, yes please. I'd love to take you up on your offer.'

'Great,' Alex said, clapping his hands together. Wolf gave a little yelp and leapt to his feet. We both laughed, breaking the tension.

'So you don't live on the premises yourself?'

'No, I bought a cottage just down the road a few years back. Everyone keeps saying you have to own property, don't they? So that's what I did—I took the plunge and signed up to a lifetime of debt.'

'Still, must be nice. Having your own place, I mean.'

I, Daisy Monroe, currently had about as much chance of owning my own house as flying to the moon.

'Yeah. It's great. You're right; I shouldn't grumble.'

'Grumble away,' I said. 'Go for it.'

Alex smiled again. 'First things first, let's get you fixed up. Daisy, if you'd care to follow me…'

'Sounds like a plan.'

Eleven

'The café's just there.' He pointed it out as we clattered up another spiral staircase. This place was like an Escher print—normal laws of gravity need not apply.

'We closed it early today. Not much trade, we're a bit short-handed at the moment, but I can bring you up some homemade soup if you like?'

Boy did I.

We arrived on the landing of the first floor. Alex felt around to his right and flicked the light switch on, but the shaded bulb didn't do much to scatter the gloom.

The upstairs hallway was dark and a bit dreary, which triggered another flurry of misgivings. Alex seemed nice and there was no doubt he was attractive. Didn't mean he wasn't planning to…oh I don't know, whatever it was serial killers did to foolish young ladies who blithely followed them up dark flights of stairs. If this was a horror movie, I'd definitely be the first one to get it.

As I dawdled a few steps behind Alex, Wolf came up behind me and butted the back of my calves, giving me an encouraging nudge.

'Some friend you are,' I muttered, reaching down to tug his ears.

'What's that?' Alex said over his shoulder.

'Oh, nothing. I was just chatting with Wolf here.'

'Right. Well, here we are. The royal suite awaits you.'

With a little ceremonial bow, he pushed the door back and invited me to enter. By that point I was too knackered to flee anyway – axe murderer or not – and so I dragged myself forwards for a peek.

The attic room was much better than I had hoped, brightly lit and spotlessly clean with large south-facing bay windows. A king-sized bed graced the near wall and antique furniture was much in evidence—an oak desk, a Narnia-style wardrobe, a plush chaise longue in one corner. And through the open door at the far end, I could see the corner of what might have been a roll-top bath. Oh God, a bath!

Stepping inside, I went over to the window and checked the scenery. Directly below, a stretch of canal wound past, bordered by a tree-lined path. Behind it, a clutch of scenic hilltops lay off in the middle distance. It was all a delightful surprise after the gloomy hallway.

Alex stayed by the door. 'Well, this is it,' he said. 'Feel free to make yourself at home. It's not much, but I hope it will do for one night.'

'It's great,' I said. 'Perfect. I can't thank you enough.'

It really was perfect. Finally, I felt a little of the weight of the day slip away. This wasn't the answer to my problems, not by a long shot, but it felt like a moment of calm in the eye of a storm. Somewhere I could finally stop and process in safety.

Alex's playful smile reappeared. 'You can thank me by having some soup.'

'Well,' I said, 'I guess I could manage that…if there's some left over?'

'Plenty,' he said. 'Just needs reheating. It'll only take a tick. I've got to finish closing up first though. Chill out for a bit, get settled in. Have a bath if you like, it's just through there—please, feel free.'

With that further kindness, and one last smile, Alex turned and left.

Twelve

Listening to the sound of Alex's retreating footsteps,
I went over to the door and locked it from the inside.
My instincts had been a little off recently, especially if
today's bolts from the blue were anything to judge by.
But right now I felt that Alex was as kind and genuine
as he appeared to be. So locking the door wasn't so
much to protect me from him as to create a barrier
against the outside world. It felt good to turn the key
and shut myself off from this totally crappy day.

Alone in the quiet, I let out a breath I didn't know
I'd been holding. I kicked off my shoes and stood
there for a moment, wondering what to do next.

Then I padded over to the bed and sank onto it. I
put my head in my hands and sat. Thinking nothing.
Just breathing.

Finally, I looked over at the bathroom. The claw-
footed tub called out to me. A nice long soak was

definitely on the agenda. I didn't need telling twice. But before I poured the water, I knew there was a phone call I had to make. I pulled my phone from my handbag and reluctantly switched it back on.

Oh boy. I had missed several calls from Mum. It was unusual for her to call me twice in one day, let alone half a dozen times. I'd planned to ring her to let her know I was safe, on the off-chance Phil had gotten in touch and told her what was going on. Seeing the string of missed calls, one after the other, removed any doubt. *She knows!*

Phil hadn't called me. I wasn't sure if this was sensible on his part or just plain insulting. He probably thought the whole thing would blow over if he gave me a day or two to come to my senses. In the meantime, he'd enlisted Mum.

That couldn't have been an easy conversation. At least that was my first thought. But then I remembered Phil's way with words and the fact he could do no wrong in Mum's eyes. After their little chat, they'd probably reached the conclusion that the problem lay with me. I didn't suppose she'd be shy in telling me so either. Right now I really didn't want to hear it.

For a moment I considered simply texting and switching the phone back off. I sighed. Best to just get it over with.

I questioned myself. Could I ever find a way to forgive Phil? At that moment I couldn't even think about it. All I could see in my mind was him and Frannie entwined passionately. A flashback that made me want to puke.

I realised that no one knew I'd also lost my job. Not even Phil. I was totally stuck. No job, no home, no boyfriend. Ruby was away travelling. Two months wages, which was all I had left, wasn't going to last long. I was basically homeless. That was what it had come to. After waking ready to accept a shiny new promotion, I'd ended the day taking refuge in a stranger's flat. In Derbyshire, of all places. Deepest, darkest Derbyshire. Thinking back on how positive I'd felt that morning, the staggering plummet was hard to swallow.

I had nothing. Unless I went back to Phil. If he even wanted me back. The thought pierced my heart and I reeled from the sudden shock of it. I hadn't even considered the possibility that this separation might work both ways. I'd assumed he'd be contrite, full of regret. But I didn't know how serious this thing with Francesca was. God, how long had it been going on? Was this the first time? Maybe Phil saw it as a blessing. Now that I finally knew, he could drop the pretence and stop sneaking around behind my back. Maybe he and Frannie would move in together, make themselves a love nest. The thought filled me with a spiralling, sick dread. I had to know either way.

With shaking hands, I swiped through my

contacts and dialled Mum's number. She picked up on the second ring.

'Daisy, is that you?'

'Hi Mum,' I said, my voice flat. I realised again how drained I was.

'Daisy, where on earth are you? We've been worried sick.'

'We?'

'I've had Phillip on the phone,' Mum said. 'He's absolutely frantic with worry.' I summoned the will to respond, my heart already sinking at her tone, but she kept talking. 'Sweetheart, you can't just disappear like this,' Mum said. 'I don't know about you, but that was *not* the way *I* was raised.'

'*Really*, Mum?' I said, almost amused. 'Did Phillip tell you what happened?'

'Of course he did. He's behaved quite appallingly, but you have to give him that, Daisy. He's man enough to own his mistakes.'

'I don't even know how to respond to that.'

'These things happen in relationships, darling. People get too comfortable. Stop making an effort. And well, Daisy, some women...they just have to work a little harder than others to keep their man interested. Unfair, I know. But true.'

My chest felt tight. 'Please Mum, can't you just support me for once? Fight my corner instead of giving me frankly insulting advice?'

My voice wobbled. I hated how weak it sounded. I was furious to find my eyes welling up yet again.

'Oh Daisy,' Mum said, 'this is a big part of the problem; you've always been so sensitive. It's like you wilfully misinterpret me. I've spoken to my friends about this, you know. And my therapist.'

Oh yes, the mythical therapist. Not a very good one if you ask me.

'Anyway, they all agree that I can't just give, give, give and get nothing back. It has to be a two-way street. Besides, if a mother can't be honest with her daughter, I don't know who can.'

From the depths of my awful misery, I summoned the will to reply. 'I need somewhere to stay,' I said, cutting her off. There was a pause at the end of the line.

'Mum?'

'Daisy, love, you have that beautiful home with Phillip.'

'I can't go back there, not right now,' I said. Another long pause. *She's going to make me ask.*

'I thought I could come and stay with you and Gerald, just for a little while.' As I heard myself say this, I realised how desperate I must be. I could hardly think of a worse shelter from the storm than their semi in Chiswick. The endless lectures I'd have to listen to. The constant recap of my faults and failings as a daughter, a girlfriend. A bloody office temp!

What were my options though? I didn't appear to have any. Plus, the small childish part of me just wanted her to offer. To tell me to come back home, even though it wasn't my home, not really.

It was a crazy idea at heart, a sign of my desperation. For one thing, it would mean me disturbing Gerald's vast rail network. He'd recently taken over the spare room, as well as the basement, and built himself a replica of the Trans-Pennine route. I couldn't see either one of them allowing me to camp out there in close proximity. There was always the danger I'd roll over and accidentally crush Huddersfield Station during the night.

There was silence on the other end of the line. 'Mum, are you still there?'

'Yes dear,' Mum said. 'It's just that I really think you ought to go back home and try to sort this out with Phillip as soon as possible, especially if this woman has got her hooks into him. They're only going to sink in deeper the longer you leave it.' Suddenly it felt like all the air was being slowly sucked out of the room. 'Don't cede the home ground is what I'm saying. You need to stand firm. Be resolute. Take it on the chin if you have to.'

'But Mum…' I said.

'Especially with a man like Phil. I mean you don't want to give up that lovely house, do you? All the benefits that relationship brings—do I really need to spell them out for you? Think about where you were before you met him. Do you really want to go back?'

I sighed and curled up on the bed, letting the phone flop onto the pillow. As usual, my participation was not required in the conversation. My heart ached. Everything ached.

'It's okay, Mum,' I said, picking up the phone again. 'I'll find somewhere. Don't you worry about me.'

'Can't you stay at Ruby's?'

'Sure,' I said. 'I'll do that.'

'Well then, there we go. Problem solved. And don't forget what I told you. If you have any sense, you'll make your way home in the morning.'

'Mum, my battery's going to die,' I said, although this didn't make the slightest bit of difference at her end. She was still talking, and telling me where I'd gone wrong, when I finally hung up.

The definition of insanity—doing the same thing over and over and expecting different results. That was the very definition of my relationship with my mother.

After putting the phone down, I racked my brain and tried to review my remaining options. As far as I could tell, there weren't a great many left to review. Going back to Phil was the smartest thing to do, according to Mum. But it didn't feel all that smart. What would it say about me – about us – if all I did was sweep his infidelity under the carpet and let bygones be bygones? Mum wanted me to be hard-headed and realistic, but that approach seemed more cowardly than anything. To pretend it was all just a lot of fuss over nothing. To keep calm and carry on. At the same time, my mum had a point—I really didn't want my old life back, living in a string of crummy apartments with cranky housemates, unable to get a moment's peace. As for relationships, I'd had boyfriends before, but Phil was an improvement on all of them. Even now, after what he'd just done.

I sighed, way beyond exhausted. My body ached like I'd just run a marathon. Remembering Alex's offer, I padded over in my stockinged feet to check out the en suite bath.

The bathroom was small, quaint, and dotted with scented candles that smelt vaguely floral. The tub itself was ornate, curving elegantly at the rim, and big enough to wallow in. A tiny cluster of essential oils were lined up next to the taps. I turned the right tap on and within seconds I heard the hot water tank rumble into action.

I couldn't think of anything better right now than a long, hot bath, except perhaps living in a parallel universe where none of this had ever happened. One in which I'd returned home to my non-cheating boyfriend to celebrate my slightly-less-imaginary promotion.

I ran the bath, good and deep, until the room filled

with steam and I could no longer see my stricken, bruised-looking eyes in the bathroom mirror. I ran lavender scented bath oil under the hot tap and swished it with my hand, testing the temperature. Then I stripped off that damned skirt suit, shed my tights and underwear and sank into the scented water with a sigh.

I closed my eyes, my mind drifting. As I was eased by the warm, fragrant water, I began to sink into a light, dreamy sleep.

Thirteen

Someone was knocking insistently on the door. I sat up sharply, sloshing water. The bath around me had gone ice cold. I realised the knocking had been going on for some time, intruding into my dream.

I lifted my hands out of the water and turned them around. My fingers looked like shrivelled prunes. The knock came again, harder this time.

'Daisy?' It was Alex, sounding worried. Oh God, he probably thought I'd done something stupid. From the hallway, I heard him shout out, 'Daisy! Are you all right?'

Embarrassed, I leapt out of the bath and grabbed the first towel I could find, yelling, 'Hold on, hold on, I'm coming,' as I skidded across the floor. I flung open the door, puffing and shedding water.

Alex stood there gawping at me. His eyes brushed

against the top of my collarbone; then he made a point of glancing away.

'Oh,' he said. 'Sorry, Daisy.'

Oh shit, I realised too late that the towel I had snatched up in my haste barely covered my—well. I crossed my legs.

'Hi,' I said brightly, puffing an errant curl away from my eyes while I slowly dripped onto the hardwood floor.

Alex was holding a tray that seemed absurdly dainty in his large hands. He thrust it towards me, still staring off at the door frame, but I was in no position to take it. If I let go of this damned towel, it was going to drop at his feet. Then we really would have something to be embarrassed about.

'Maybe you could put it down over there,' I said, gesturing in the general direction of the bedside table with one hand while the other kept the towel scrunched together.

'Right, okay.' Alex marched across the room. Determinedly not looking at me, he put the tray down where I'd asked him to. I edged a little closer. Something smelt wonderful.

'Soup,' Alex said. Oh God, now he actually had his hand half over his eyes, the poor man. Here he was trying to do me a simple favour and I'd turned him into an accidental Peeping Tom!

The corner of my mouth crept up an inch. There

was something quite endearing about seeing this six-foot-something Man (with a capital M) in such a fluster.

Bending down as carefully as I could, I breathed in the aromatic scent while trying not to reveal what little of me was still left to my host's imagination. 'That smells amazing,' I said. 'Did you make this as well?'

Alex nodded from behind his hand mask. 'Pastry chef, short order cook, odd job man, and bookseller on a good day. You get to wear a lot of hats around here. It's one of the benefits of being chronically short-staffed.'

'You can tell it's home-made,' I told him. 'Clearly prepared with lots of love.'

This pleased Alex enough for him to chance a peek in my general direction. I smiled encouragingly at him and gave the inviting bowl another sniff.

'Mm…Chicken soup, my favourite,' I said.

'You arrived on a good day then.' Alex's fingers widened again and he chanced another look in my direction. I felt a darting pull in my stomach as our eyes connected. I completely forgot we were chatting about soup. The smile promptly dropped off my face. Oh boy.

'I brought you some clothes as well,' he said. 'Just a T-shirt to sleep in.' His voice seemed to have dropped an octave, sending a shiver across my skin.

From the slight upward twitch of his lips, I'd say he had noticed my reaction. My cheeks heated with embarrassment.

'Right-oh,' I said. *Right-oh? Sweet Jesus, who am I, Mary F-ing Poppins?* I felt a giggle bubbling up inside me. The towel slipped an inch and I grabbed at it wildly.

'Right, right,' Alex said. I snorted. Suddenly, Alex held his hand up to his mouth, laughing into it, trying not to look at me while I rearranged myself.

The sound of his rich, rumbling voice set me off even more and I cracked up laughing as well. At least I'd dialled back the sexual tension with my goofy shenanigans.

'Sorry, Daisy,' Alex said, getting control of himself. 'I know I shouldn't laugh, but this whole situation is a bit…'

Sexy, I thought. Although I answered, 'Awkward,' instead.

'Exactly,' Alex said.

Just then I heard the familiar scrabble of nails as Wolf bounded in the room and made a beeline straight for me.

'Oh no, you don't,' Alex said, grabbing his collar as I backed away, hissing 'Bad doggy,' at Wolf, who grinned happily back at me.

'I'm not decent,' I said. 'You can't be jumping all over me at a time like this.'

Restrained at the last moment, Wolf rolled his eyes up at me.

'I better get out of your hair then,' Alex said. 'Just come down when you're ready in the morning. I'll take you to the station. I've written my number down for you. Call me if you need anything. Anything at all.'

I nodded, taking the number from him, not trusting myself to speak. Who was this man who would put himself out so thoroughly for a stranger? I tried to imagine Phil doing the same thing in a similar situation. Nope.

Maybe he was just trying to get into my pants. But other than that heated moment just gone – and let's be honest I was standing practically naked and dripping wet right in front of him – I hadn't gotten the sense that he was laying it on thick or trying it on in any way.

Alex retreated towards the door and tried taking Wolf with him. But the Great Dane dug his claws in. He clearly didn't want to go.

'Wolf. Come,' said Alex. The dog rolled his eyes up at Alex, his expression said, 'Not bloody likely.'

'It's okay, he can stay here,' I said. 'Keep watch over me.'

'I should warn you, he snores,' Alex said.

'So do I,' I answered.

Alex laughed. 'Can you leave the door open a

crack if he's still here when you go to bed? Otherwise he'll be scratching at the door and bothering you in the night. He's got a doggy flap downstairs so he can get out if he needs to.'

'Sure thing,' I nodded.

'Okay, get some rest, Daisy,' Alex added, his voice gentle now. 'Things will look better in the morning.'

'I'm not so sure about that.'

Alex shot me another of those concerned looks as if my well-being really mattered to him. There was a slightly awkward pause.

'Well, goodnight then,' he said, and left, shutting the door behind him.

I looked down at Wolf, who looked back at me as if to say, 'So…now what?' He trotted over to the foot of the bed and settled down on the floor. He put his muzzle on his paw with a huff of air.

I made a beeline for the goodies Alex had left me. Holy mackerel, it really did look good. A deep bowl of steaming chicken broth and three slices of thick bread slathered in creamy butter. Nor had Alex stopped there. There was cheese and crackers with home-made pickle on a side dish. A big mug of tea. And bless your soul, St. Alex of Upper Fingly – or wherever the hell it was I'd washed up – a miniature bottle of cabernet.

Also on the tray my host had placed the offending copy of Poe's *Collected Works* that had conked me on the head earlier. I could chuckle about it now, which surely counted as progress.

On the bed neatly folded was an oversized man's T-shirt. I picked it up and gave it a sniff, rather disappointed to find that it smelled of laundry detergent, not—not what? *Daisy, you shameless perv.* I pushed my smutty thoughts away.

Planting myself on the bed, I picked the spoon up and made short work of the chicken broth. Wolf flopped at my feet, making puppy eyes and throwing in the odd mournful whine for good measure. After I'd demolished a good four-fifths of it, I relented and put the bowl down next to my suddenly animated companion.

While Wolf licked the bowl clean, I changed into my borrowed nightshirt. The one that Alex normally filled out with his broad shoulders and rippling six-pack. *For goodness' sake, Daisy, enough now!*

Switching off the main light, I flicked on the antique lamp with the frilly shade that stood on the bedside table. Then I slipped beneath the covers and twisted open the miniature bottle of red wine. Drinking straight from the bottle, I flicked through the Poe book. In the mood for something suitably dark and brooding, I settled on 'The Tell-Tale Heart'.

If Wolf did snore, I wasn't aware of it. Within twenty minutes I had fallen into a deep, dreamless sleep, the book still in my hand. At some point in the night, the great galah got onto the bed and tunnelled his way up under the covers. I wrapped myself around him, breathing in his warm doggy smell, and cried into his fur, racked with feelings of sorrow and confusion. A sense of being all alone in the world. Lost. Then I went back to sleep and knew nothing more until the morning. In fact, I didn't wake again until the day was well and truly underway.

Fourteen

I shifted my legs and snuggled deeper into the bed. The air smelt floral and from behind my closed eyes, I could tell it was bright outside. I pulled the blanket over my head, reluctant to fully awaken. The cloth felt scratchy and unfamiliar against my cheek.

Anxiety began to gnaw. A prickle of unease. I knew something was wrong before I was awake enough to remember what it was. Then, like a sucker punch, everything came flooding back.

Getting fired, fleeing from Phil and Francesca. My breakdown on the tube.

My eyes popped open. I wasn't in London. I was… actually I still didn't know exactly where I was. Not that I was in any great rush to piece things together. I wanted nothing more than to fall back into forgetful oblivion. My eyelids started to sink. But I didn't really have that luxury. I had decisions to make. Big ones.

Like where the hell I was going to live and how the hell I was going to pay for it.

I slowly rolled the blanket down until my eyes were peeping out over the top. The room was bright, sunlight playing on the walls. I must have fallen asleep without even drawing the curtains. Now the sun beamed cheerfully through the window, directly into my face. I scowled back at it.

Realising I was always going to be the loser in that particular battle, I fumbled for my phone, blearily rubbing the sleep out of my eyes, then sat bolt upright when I saw what time it was.

The veil of sleep promptly dropped away and I was left with cold, clean panic. Shit! I'd slept for sixteen hours straight. How was that even possible?

Oh God. My stomach dropped. I had planned to be up and ready first thing. What must Alex be thinking? Had he waited for me at breakfast? Was he pissed off? Mortified, I flopped back down on the bed.

I gave myself another few moments to fester in self-pity, but eventually my eyes drifted to the window. If the bright blue patch of sky I could see was anything to judge by, it was a beautiful day. I sighed. I couldn't lie here feeling sorry for myself much longer. I was going to have to go downstairs and face the music.

The dog had left me at some point in the night and I wondered if I had dreamt him up. Then I sneezed.

I picked a grey hair off my shoulder. Nope. Wolf was real all right.

I glanced back at my phone. No more missed calls, but several texts had come in from Phil during the night, the last around 11:00 p.m. I'd slept right through them all. I scrolled through as they went from apologetic to irritated. The last one simply said, *Please call me, Daisy. This is childish. We need to talk. You owe me that much.*

I put the phone back on the bedside table, rather more forcefully than was strictly necessary. Okay, maybe my response yesterday had been a little extreme, but he didn't get to call me out on things anymore. He'd lost that right. Rather than being empowering, the thought sat heavy in my chest, making me feel sad and defeated. Alone. I was totally alone.

What was I supposed to do—swallow my pride, suck it up, pretend that none of this had happened? According to my mum at least, the answer was yes.

You owe me that much…

I stared again at the last line of his text message. I didn't see how I could possibly owe Phil anything after what had happened yesterday. I heard Mum's reply to that, as if she was right here in the room and leaning into my ear.

What about that lovely flat, Daisy? The enviable life you lead. All those little luxuries you've grown accustomed to.

Which was all true, but what was that life worth

if it was built on deception? I knew that Phil was completely dependable in other ways, but surely this was the one that really mattered? Or was Mum right? Were these just the fanciful notions of a sensitive dreamer, an incurable romantic?

Pursing my lips, I picked the phone up again and made my decision. Whether I owed Phil a call or not, I owed it to myself to be assertive. Whatever happened next, I needed to get out on the front foot instead of hiding away. That said, I stayed in bed to make the call, propped up against the pillows, with the blankets draped over me like armour.

I listened to the call signal, my heart in my mouth. Phil answered on the fourth ring.

'Daisy. At last. Thank God.'

The worry was clear in his voice, and, despite myself, I felt relieved to hear it. I steeled myself. Phil didn't need to know what I was feeling.

'Well,' I said instead, 'here I am, what do you have to say for yourself?'

'Where to start?' he said. 'To say I've been a fool would be an understatement.'

'Then how about we label you a stupid prick instead?'

That left Phil speechless. I was a little taken aback myself by the sudden flare of anger.

'Okay. Yes, if you must. A stupid prick. I can hardly argue with that, can I?'

I knew what it cost Phil to show that much humility.

'I did catch you bang to rights.'

'I can explain though,' he said. 'Okay, not all of it. But you have to hear me out and let me put the whole thing into context.'

'Be my guest,' I said. 'I'm all ears.'

'It doesn't excuse everything, I know, but Frannie really did throw herself at me.'

'You didn't seem to be putting up much of a fight.'

'She ambushed me, babe. Honestly! One minute we were talking normally, and the next she was all over me.'

'None of which explains why you were at home in the middle of the day, all alone with your "attacker".' I injected as much sarcasm as I could into that last word.

'I know it looks bad, Goose, but I do have an explanation. She said she had to see me. Claimed it couldn't wait. Evidently, she'd had the most terrible bust-up with Sebastian that morning and there was no one else she could turn to. I know in hindsight it looks dodgy as hell, but what else was I supposed to do?'

'So you want me to believe you were just being a good Samaritan?'

'Yes,' Phil said. 'Exactly. It wasn't like I wanted to get caught in the middle. Sebastian's a good friend. And I'd always thought that Fran was too.'

'Oh, she's friendly all right…'

'I know,' Phil agreed. 'The thing is I've never thought much of it before—the way she can get a little touchy-feely. I just thought that's how she was with everyone.'

'Not really.'

'Well, hindsight is a wonderful thing. If I'm guilty of anything it's naivety.'

'So none of this was pre-planned, is that what you're saying?'

'I swear to you, Daisy. I was as shocked as you by the way events unfolded.'

I shook my head vigorously, although Phil couldn't see me.

'I doubt that very much.'

'And it wouldn't have gone any further, if that's what you're thinking. There's no way in a million years I would have allowed that to happen. I know I didn't stop it quickly enough. Daisy, I'm truly sorry for that. It was just the shock. You know?'

I kept quiet, trying to take it all in. Was I buying this?

'I *don't* know, Phil,' I said finally. 'It all sounds pretty far-fetched.'

'I realise that, I do. But I need you to believe me, Goose. I'm telling you the truth.'

This wasn't like Phil at all. He hardly ever apologised, certainly not this profusely. I admit I felt a small thrill of power at that. I rarely held the power in our relationship. Not since the very beginning at least, when he was still pursuing me. I had always felt, deep down, that he was too good for me. I'd wondered why someone like him had chosen to love someone like me. So when I'd caught him with Frannie, it was really just a confirmation of my insecurities. That voice in your head, the one everyone says you should ignore. Turns out it was right all along.

Ordinarily, I would have started to thaw at this point. He would buy me a nice gift, shower me with flowers. And I'd cave—all would be forgiven. I hardened my heart. Not this time. This was not just some minor tiff. If I relented now, he would think that what he'd done was okay. I'd be on guard forever more.

'I need to think it over,' I said. 'Weigh up everything you've said.'

'Of course,' Phil said. 'Take another day if you need to.'

'No,' I said. 'It has to be longer than that. You can't just expect me to turn up tomorrow like everything's okay.'

'And just how long are you thinking exactly?' I could hear the irritation returning to Phil's voice. My natural impulse was to soothe it, to take the edge off, but I stood my ground.

'A month.'

'A month!'

'That's right. Time for us to reflect on things properly—what we both want from this relationship.'

There was another pause in the conversation. I could sense Phil's mind whirring. Wondering if this was the best outcome he could hope for or if he should push his luck further. 'And where are you going to stay?' he said at last. 'Can you tell me that?' His voice sounded annoyingly triumphant, like he knew I had nowhere else to go.

The pause between us grew. Just as I heard him draw breath to say something else I blurted out, 'Actually, I didn't have the time to tell you yesterday...' I paused again, not entirely sure where I was going with this.

'Yes?' said Phil. Then impatiently, 'What, Daisy? What didn't you have time to tell me?' He sounded smug. He knew I was bluffing.

'Um. The office wants me up in Derbyshire.'

'What!'

'That's right. The meeting with Oliver, that's what it was about. They're launching a new, um...a new regional branch.' Oh boy, I was getting on a bit of a roll here. 'I don't know if it's going to be permanent or not or whether they just need me to get the intranet up and running. But, well, for the next thirty days, it's all systems go.'

Phil was silent. No doubt stunned. He wasn't the only one. What the hell had I just said?

'Derbyshire?' he said doubtfully. 'Intranet? Seriously, Daisy?'

'Yep. That's where I'm calling you from now. Deepest, darkest Derbyshire.'

'Where? A hotel?'

'Err, that's right.' God, I was a terrible liar! 'I'm in the lobby right now. I have to say, it's pretty fancy. Oliver's really splashed out.'

I looked around the bookshop's upstairs room. For all its faded charm, chic it certainly wasn't. Perhaps I was a better liar than I thought.

'But you don't have any of your things.'

'Oh, that's all taken care of,' I said breezily.

'I don't know what to say,' Phil said.

'How about, "Congratulations"?'

'Yes, of course,' he said uncertainly. 'That all sounds wonderful. We'll have to have a proper celebration when you get back.'

'Before we do that, or anything else, we need to have a serious conversation about where we go from here as a couple,' I said.

'To be honest,' said Phil, 'this is something I've been meaning to talk to you about for ages. I could kick myself for not doing it before now.'

'What do you mean?' I asked, still veering between exhilaration and blind panic over the whopping great lie I'd just told.

'You and me,' he said. 'I think we should formalise

things. I don't see any point in putting it off any longer. It's time I made an honest woman of you.'

If Phil's aim was to wrong-foot me and wrest the advantage back, this massive bombshell had certainly done the trick.

'You're saying we should get married?'

'I don't want an answer now, of course,' Phil said. 'That wouldn't be fair after everything that's happened. All I'm asking is that you think about it and promise to hear me out at the end of the month.'

For another half dozen seconds, I struggled to formulate an answer. The best I could manage, utterly astonished, was a subdued, 'Okay.'

'Great,' said Phil. 'You won't regret it, Goose. We're a hell of a team, you and me.'

Fifteen

I struggled out of bed and walked in a daze to the bathroom. I splashed cold water on my face repeatedly. This did nothing to clear my head—does it ever?

I stared into the bathroom mirror at my gobsmacked reflection. I looked every bit as stunned as I felt. Had Phil really just proposed to me? Now? I'd thought nothing could top yesterday in terms of emotional upheaval. Turns out I was mistaken.

Through the floorboards directly below me, I heard the hubbub of conversation. One of these muffled voices sounded very much like Alex. I wondered if he was talking extra loudly, a little hint to get me to vacate the premises. Maybe he thought he had a squatter on his hands.

As I shuffled back into the bedroom, I laughed bleakly at my new situation. Thanks to my masterstroke in lying to Phil, I was in a worse pickle than yesterday afternoon. Instead of worrying where to spend the night, I had another twenty-nine to fret about.

It was time to get dressed and face the music. But I also needed just a little longer to compose myself. One last moment of quiet before I slunk out of the Bookshop Café and dragged myself off who knew where. To be honest, at this point, an extra few minutes wasn't going to make any real difference.

I padded across the hardwood floor over to the window and peered out across an array of assorted rooftops and pretty gardens. The canal glinted serenely at my feet, and beyond that, rolling green hills, criss-crossed with crumbling stone walls. Here and there, flocks of plump, grazing sheep.

I fiddled with the latch and pushed up, grumbling a little when it stuck. Then the window slid open in one smooth motion. In came a whoosh of clean, fresh air.

Despite how much pretty countryside Britain had to offer, I'd spent most of my life in the city, rarely venturing out of the smoggy hub. Concrete under my feet and the ragged teeth of tower blocks above. I shivered at the image. It felt good to be away from honking traffic and constantly ringing phones. Not surrounded by a million people polluting the air with their wants and desires. Just me.

I breathed in the fresh air, feeling suddenly lighter,

freer. People always said fresh air did you the world of good. Maybe they were right. As I stared out at the charming view, I tried drawing on it for inspiration. Wasn't that another benefit of beautiful scenery— putting brilliant ideas in your head? *Lord knows I've never had more need of a stroke of genius than right now.*

No one was going to sort my life out for me. Somehow, I had to do it myself. I had no idea how, but this seemed like the perfect place to start trying.

Something stirred at the back of my mind. I tried to bring it into sharper focus. What I dredged up from the murky depths was an idle comment that Alex had made last night.

'Pastry chef, short order cook, odd job man, and bookseller on a good day. You get to wear a lot of hats around here. It's one of the benefits of being chronically short-staffed.'

There you go, Daisy. A chronic staff shortage. We can't have that now, can we? Someone should ride to this lovely man's rescue. Who better than you?

I held the thought up to the light for inspection. Examined it. It wavered a little then held. Was it an inspired idea or simply bonkers? I wasn't sure, but it was the best I could come up with at such short notice. I took another look out the window, and then back at the room, and nodded. I could see myself here for a month. It wouldn't even be that much of a hardship, considering the alternatives. Now, using all my powers of persuasion – *What bloody powers?* – I had to make Alex see it too. I thought back to his easy, open manner yesterday and the kindness he'd shown me. I guess no good deed goes unpunished. I was about to put him in an incredibly awkward situation.

After making myself halfway presentable, I pulled the door back and strode out into the hallway before my determination could desert me.

As I made my way down the stairs from the attic, my resolution was slightly marred by my crazy hair and outfit of Alex's T-shirt, tucked into the bottom half of my skirt suit. Football socks and no shoes. Not necessarily the best outfit to pitch my proposition in. But I was working with what I had.

Halfway down, I realised that since I had slept until midday, the shop was likely to be full of customers. Maybe that was who I'd heard from the bathroom. I ran my hands through my hair, dithering.

'Come on, Daisy, old girl,' I said, in my best old-timey movie-star voice. 'You've got this.'

When that didn't work, I resolutely slouched my way down the stairs, girding my loins (whatever the hell that actually means).

I stood for a moment in the gallery, girding said loins, when I noticed with some amusement that the shelves where I stood were lined with books of the "adult" variety. Victorian smut. Tantric sex manuals. Lurid paperbacks from the 1970s. Sleaze of every variety catering to all manner of tastes.

I was tempted to stop for a nice long perv, but time was pressing so I pushed on further into the bookshop. Instinctively, I took a narrow corridor off to my left. Halfway along it, I realised that I was being led by my nose. The smell of cooking was wafting towards me. Suddenly I was ravenous, practically drooling.

The smell grew stronger, and eventually I found myself outside a pair of swing-doors. Behind them, I could hear the clanking of pots and pans and the sound of something bubbling. Rolling my shoulders in readiness, while rehearsing my speech a final time, I gave a little rap then pushed on into the kitchen.

Here goes nothing…

Sixteen

The kitchen was small, clean, and well-stocked with shiny utensils. A hub of bustling activity, it boasted a tall chrome fridge and an extensive gas range on which a motley array of pots and pans sizzled and simmered.

Standing behind the stove, a sandy-haired young man was busy stirring a pot full of delicious smelling red sauce. As I entered, he turned around and gave me a friendly smile. 'Hey, you must be Daisy?'

I nodded, fiddling with the hem of Alex's T-shirt, more than a little embarrassed by my appearance. 'Was it my fancy threads that gave me away?'

The young man chuckled. 'I'm Joe, by the way. Alex's brother. He just stepped outside for a sprig of parsley.'

'So you grow your own herbs too?'

'Alex does. I'm not much of a gardener myself. Not much of a cook, if I'm being honest.'

'That smells wonderful though,' I said.

He shrugged. 'I'm just keeping an eye on it. Deputising for the chief.'

I still felt more than a little shaky after the phone call with Phil, but Joe had a warm confidence about him and a steady patter of small talk that put me immediately at ease. Maybe it was a family trait.

'Fancy a cuppa?'

I smiled at him gratefully and nodded, sinking onto a wooden stool. He poured out a mug of steaming hot tea and brought it over to me. I blew on it, just about to take a sip when the back door opened and Alex came in.

'Daisy. You're up!'

I blushed. This didn't exactly fill me with confidence. I wondered, with a sinking heart, if he expected me to push off straight away.

I gave him a timid smile. Dear God, he was good looking. I had wondered if yesterday's events, combined with the bump on the head, had clouded my judgement. But no, this morning he looked even better, if that was possible. He was clean shaven, and just to really top things off he had a cute little smudge of flour across the bridge of his nose and dusted through his hair.

Turning to his brother, Alex nodded at the stove. 'Those should be ready now, Joe.'

After giving a playful salute, Joe scooped a dozen

or so plump, fluffy dumplings out of the boiling pan of water with a slotted spoon before sliding them into a pan of sizzling brown butter.

I drifted closer. 'What is that?' I asked, gesturing at the pan. 'It smells amazing.'

'Gnocchi,' said Alex from the counter opposite, rolling out an oblong of dough before deftly cutting it into small pieces about the size of a wine cork. He crimped one with the edge of a fork and held it up to show me. 'Basically, potato dumplings,'

At the same time, Joe was busy spooning copious amounts of butter over the gnocchi, as they slowly turned golden in the pan. My mouth watered as I watched the brothers in action. The smell in the kitchen was out of this world.

'These are done,' Joe said, mixing in the tomato sauce.

'Would you mind taking them out to table three?'

'Sure,' he said, balancing plates carefully in both hands.

My eyes hungrily followed Joe out of the kitchen.

'Hungry?' Alex said.

Damn it. Wolf had more self-control than I did right now. I rolled my tongue back up into my mouth and tried not to wag my tail.

'I couldn't possibly,' I demurred.

'How about some toast? We've got homemade jam,' he said, waggling his eyebrows.

'Well…maybe just a slice. If you're not too busy?'

'Not at all. The lunch time rush is pretty much over.'

'Go on then,' I said. 'You've twisted my arm.' If nothing else, it bought me a little more time to say my piece.

'So, did you sleep well?' Alex asked, slicing the yummy-looking bread into thick slices.

'I'm really sorry,' I said, 'I never usually sleep this late. I don't know what came over me.'

'Well, you had quite the day yesterday. You probably needed a little extra rest.'

'Little!' I said. 'You're kidding, aren't you? It's already past midday!'

Alex laughed. He popped two slices of bread into the toaster then came and sat across from me at the small table. He studied me intently.

'You look better,' he said. 'A lot less flustered.'

'Don't you believe it,' I told him.

'Your troubles haven't gone away then?'

'Nope. They've stuck around. One or two of them have even deepened.'

Alex nodded sympathetically. 'That's troubles for you. They're clingy bastards, aren't they?'

I could feel my bottom lip about to wobble again, so I bit into it and changed the subject completely. 'If you don't mind me asking, who's out front, minding the bookshop?'

'Ah, that would be no one,' Alex said. 'Although we do have the bell over the door and one on the counter, if anyone needs serving. I can normally hear its tinkle out back.'

'Hardly ideal,' I said.

'Not really,' Alex admitted. 'Janice comes in two days a week, but there's not much call for her on Tuesdays. It's normally pretty dead.'

'So, no full-time shop assistant, chef, waiter?'

Alex shook his head. 'To be honest, we don't have a full-time anything, barring me. Joe helps out when he can, but he's got a dissertation to write and I can't ask him to do any more than he already does.

'Janice is great, but unfortunately she's moving away from the area shortly, which is going to…well, you don't need to worry about that.'

I took another sip of tea then set my mug down on the table. If there was ever a good moment to put myself forward, this seemed to be it.

I mustered my courage, sat up straight and plastered on a confident smile. 'Clearly, what you need to do is find someone reliable and enthusiastic who can hit the ground running…' I paused for dramatic effect.

Alex leaned back in his chair and studied me. 'Hmm…you wouldn't happen to know anyone who fits that description?' he said.

'As a matter of fact, I do.' I lifted a finger and tapped it against my collarbone. 'This guy,' I said cockily. 'Well, um…I mean, girl…obviously.' *Dammit, I need to work on my one-liners.*

Alex's smile brightened. 'You want to work here?'

'For a month,' I said. 'If you'll have me. You won't regret it, I promise.'

'No,' he said, beaming broadly. 'I don't suppose I would.'

'Great. Fantastic. I'll start straight away.'

Alex frowned. 'Hang on, slow down a minute.'

Dammit—so close. Alex went over to the counter, catching the toast just as the toaster popped.

'That could be tricky. We have a bit of a cash-flow situation at the moment. I'm not sure we could afford to pay you.'

'Oh,' I said, relieved that this was his only objection. 'I was thinking I could work for room and board.' Alex popped the plate down in front of me.

'Well, how about it?' I asked around a mouthful of toast.

Alex's frown had disappeared. 'That sounds pretty great.'

I stuck my hand out again and gave it a little waggle, encouraging him to shake on it. Following my example, Alex gripped my palm, holding it a little longer than was strictly business-like, which was perfectly okay with me.

As we were doing so, Joe returned to the kitchen with a stack of empty plates and caught the tail-end of our agreement. 'Hello, hello,' he said. 'What devilish bargain have you struck now, big brother?'

Alex turned to him and presented me. 'Say hello to our new member of staff.'

'Really?' Joe said. He seemed almost as pleased as his sibling by the sudden development.

'Yep,' said Alex. 'Daisy will be with us for the next month, staying in the attic room.'

'Does this mean I'll get the odd afternoon off now?' Joe asked hopefully.

'We'll see,' Alex said.

Joe rolled his eyes. 'Careful my brother doesn't work you to death,' he said, laughing.

'I'll go and take over the shop counter then, should I?' I said, hopping up from the bench, eager to prove myself.

Alex held his hand out, halting me in my tracks. 'Tomorrow's fine. Take the afternoon to get your bearings. I don't know, maybe you want to buy a few basics?' he said, eyeing my eccentric outfit. 'You can go and sample the delights of Upper Finlay.'

'That should take you all of five minutes,' said Joe.

'I'm sure that's not true,' I said. 'It looks like it has oodles of charm to me.'

'I was just thinking with you being a city girl you might struggle with the sleepy pace.'

'Bring it on,' I said. 'The sleepier the better. I could do with a break from all the madness.'

'Oh well,' said Alex, smiling again, 'you might just have come to the right place.'

'I'll see you tomorrow then?' I said. 'What time do you want me downstairs?'

Alex rose from the table and took my plate over to the sink. Lazy hound that I am, I let him.

'I was thinking I'd see you tonight. You'll need a proper induction before I let you loose on the shop floor. We can do that while I feed you.'

'There's no need to go to any trouble.'

'You did say room *and* board, didn't you? I have to hold up my side of the bargain.'

'I'm quite happy to settle for leftovers, especially if that yummy chicken soup was anything to go by.'

Alex shook his head firmly. 'Uh, uh. No way. A deal's a deal, especially as I'm not actually going to be paying you. I feel bad enough about that as it is.'

'Well, in that case…'

'Good. There we are then.' It was his turn to jump the gun and act like everything was settled. 'I'll meet you back here in the kitchen at seven. That should give you plenty of time to acclimatise.' He grinned. 'You're going to need it.'

'I'll say,' Joe chipped in.

'I take it you get more than your fair share of local eccentrics then?'

'Weirdos,' Alex said. 'Let's not beat around the bush.'

I chuckled at the claim. 'Oh well, I guess I'd better go meet and greet them.'

'Good luck,' said Joe, smirking as he washed dishes in the sink.

Off in the distance, we heard the faint tinkle of a bell.

'A customer!' said Alex. 'On a Tuesday. That counts as a minor miracle. Daisy, you must be a good luck charm.'

I responded by giving him a goofy grin. I couldn't remember anyone ever calling me *that* before.

Seventeen

I went out the back door and round the side of the bookshop, trying to remember the directions Alex had given me. Not that there was any danger, he'd said, of me getting lost in Upper Finlay.

According to Alex, I had encountered the high street already on my way from the train station. I couldn't remember seeing anything that fitted that description. Just a small huddle of shops either side of the pub that I'd hurried past.

I soon found myself opposite that same pub. It seemed friendlier today, although that was probably more to do with my improved state of mind than anything else. On the benches outside sat a trio of pensioners enjoying the sunshine and half pints of dark ale.

I span around on my heel, unsure where to go next.

'You all right, duck? You're not lost, are you?'

It was one of the pensioners who spoke up, a woman who looked to be in her early seventies. She was wearing a huge baggy jumper, two sizes too big, and sported a glorious bouffant of lilac-tinted hair.

I turned around, smiling, and considered her question. 'The high street,' I said uncertainly. 'I don't suppose you could tell me where it is?'

This prompted laughter from all three of them, although it seemed light-hearted enough.

'You're looking at it,' said the only gent, a man with an astonishing rockabilly pompadour. It was dyed jet back, slicked at the sides, and rose from his forehead in a great elaborate crest. He stretched his arms out in both directions. 'Here it is. Right before your eyes. The whole shopping experience.'

'Okay,' I said. 'Thanks.'

'Not local then,' said the second elderly woman. It was a fact, not a question.

'No,' I said. 'Just visiting.'

'For the day?' asked the ageing rocker.

'A month by the looks of things. I'm helping out in the bookshop for a little while.'

'Ah well, I'm sure they'll be grateful for that,' said the first woman.

'By the way,' I said, 'I don't suppose you could point me in the direction of a pound shop?'

I was hoping to God Upper Finlay had one, given the money I had left.

'Sorry, love. That would be a no,' the old woman with the lilac hair said.

'Okay. Thanks anyway,' I answered.

'There's always TCFCTSI,' she added. 'That's about the closest thing we have to a discount store. If you're wanting a bargain, that would be your best bet.'

'TCFCTSI?'

I wasn't sure if this was a tortured acronym or some strange Derbyshire slang word.

'Two doors down on your left,' she said, nodding towards the curiously named outlet. 'You can't miss it.'

I said goodbye to my new acquaintances and another thirty steps took me to the shop front. There it was – TCFCTSI – stencilled across the door. There were mannequins in the window, male and female, all wearing Hawaiian shirts and tracksuit bottoms, striking strange dramatic poses.

Pushing the door open, I walked in and took a few steps forward. It was a charity shop. An especially cluttered one, crammed with second-hand goods of every description. As I sought out women's clothes among the jumbled chaos, a man appeared from nowhere and slid alongside me.

'Good afternoon, madam. Welcome to our little emporium. May I be of assistance in any way?'

He was wearing a shiny grey suit and looked like an insurance salesman from a much earlier decade.

I was too startled to answer immediately. Instead I studied the name tag clipped to his shiny lapel, which identified him as GEOFF.

I shook my head, retreating half a step. 'Just browsing.'

Geoff advanced, reclosing the gap between us. 'Would that be for clothes, records, knickknacks? As you can see, we cover all the product categories.' Geoff looked around the place, radiating pride at this wide selection of goods.

'It's very impressive,' I said, not knowing how else to answer.

He nodded, accepting the compliment. 'We do like to think so, me and Auntie Lou.'

Geoff gestured towards the far corner of the shop, which housed a giant Lazy Boy armchair. A tiny, ancient woman with a face like a wrinkled prune reclined casually on it, eating an overripe banana. She was wrapped in a brightly coloured poncho, her slipper-clad feet up on the extended footrest. Her eyes were glued to a paperback copy of *Fifty Shades of Grey*.

'Blimey,' she said, pausing to fold down the corner of one page. She licked her finger and used it to turn on to the next.

Her eyes scanned the page. 'Blimey,' she said again.

Thinking it was probably best to leave her to

it I turned back to Geoff and, against my better judgement, asked the obvious question.

'So…TCFCTSI?'

Geoff nodded vigorously. Although he must have been asked this question hundreds of times, he clearly wasn't tired of giving the answer. 'That, my dear, would be The Charity for Career Threatening Sports Injuries.'

I tried my best to suppress a laugh. 'Right. I see.'

'Now, I know what you're going to say,' Geoff continued, 'that we lack the gravitas of the likes of Oxfam, the British Heart Foundation, and the Red Cross.' His voice dripped venom as he spoke of his rivals. 'But let me set you straight, life is no picnic for those lads and lasses with ruptured ligaments and worn tendons.' He wagged a finger in my general direction, 'and don't get me started on golfer's knee.'

I straightened my face, trying to supress the giggle I felt bubbling up. 'Golfer's knee,' I said, 'tragic.'

'Quite,' Geoff said, tutting.

Auntie Lou managed to drag her eyes away from *Fifty Shades*. She rolled them at Geoff's earnestness. Then, not breaking my gaze, she tossed the banana skin over her left shoulder, where it landed with astonishing accuracy in a small round bin. She gave me a toothless grin and went back to reading her smutty paperback. Auntie Lou was a badass!

I spied a cluster of clothes rails to my left and

made a move towards them. 'There we are,' I said. 'Women's clothes. I'll just have a quick look if that's all right?'

'Of course,' said Geoff, following me closely. *Bloody hell, Geoff,* I thought, *give a girl some space.* 'Take all the time you need. As you can see, we have garments for every occasion.'

I grabbed several items off the rails.

'Is there a changing room I could use?'

'There to your right,' he said. 'I think you'll find it meets your requirements.'

I retreated into it and drew the curtains firmly closed behind me. Slipping out of my ropey attire, I ran through several costume changes, admiring myself shamelessly in the mirror.

I used to be something of a charity shop addict before I met Phil. It was a style that Phil claimed to like – 'very boho' – although he soon put a stop to it, buying me an entire new wardrobe from the same expensive boutiques frequented by his friends' wives and girlfriends. When I'd suggested that this was a bit over the top, he'd answered, 'Come on now, Goose. You want to fit in, don't you?'

As if that was ever going to happen. But I let it go, as usual. It actually felt pretty good to let my own tastes run riot, however quirky. The only problem was that, even though the clothes were fairly cheap, the total was still considerably more than I wanted to spend. I felt a twinge of anxiety about delving into my paltry savings. Well, I couldn't live for a month in a soiled skirt suit and Alex's old T-shirt. I had to suck it up.

I swished through the curtains clutching my spoils and made for the counter, hoping to sweet talk Geoff into a discount. Geoff stood behind it, waiting expectantly.

'You found something then?' he said. 'I knew you would.' He eyed me sternly as he said this, as though I might have been busy spreading rumours to the contrary. 'Very few customers ever leave here empty-handed.'

I put the clothes down and smiled at him hopefully. 'I don't suppose you could drop the price a little?'

He looked at me aghast, as though I had just suggested we rob a bank together. Bonnie and Clyde – Daisy and Geoff – it had a certain ring to it.

'I'd like to, young lady. I really would. But if word got out…well, everyone would want a discount, wouldn't they? You see my problem?'

'Um…no…'

'Look on the bright side,' he said. 'Our nation's proud sportsmen and woman will be thankful for your help.'

Given the wretched state of my finances, this wasn't much of a consolation.

A high, creaky voice interrupted our negotiations.

'Oh, for goodness' sake, lad. Just call it a tenner.'

We both looked over at Auntie Lou, who looked back, her expression brooking no argument. She nodded her head with an air of finality. 'Yup, a tenner should do it.'

'But Auntie Lou…' Geoff said, his voice rising by an octave. She lifted an eyebrow and left it there, until Geoff backed down with a *humph*. Auntie Lou was a lady of few words, but when she spoke, it obviously counted.

Shaking his head, Geoff began to fold the pile of clothes I'd dropped on the counter, taking longer, I felt, than was strictly necessary. Once he'd finished, he popped them in a bag for me. I handed over a ten-pound note, which he took with the tips of his fingers like it was a poisonous scorpion.

'That'll be five pence for the bag, please.' I handed over a five pence piece and he dropped it into the till victoriously. *Whatever gets you through the day, Geoffrey*, I thought.

I practically bounced out of the shop. I hadn't done much for the nation's injured athletes, admittedly, but I'd never haggled successfully before. Even with Auntie Lou's intervention, it felt like a minor triumph.

'Thank you, Auntie Lou,' I said as I was leaving. She raised a hand in acknowledgement but didn't look up from the smut.

Eighteen

After returning to my little attic room. I had a marathon soak in the tub, topping up with hot water until I was more pruney than Auntie Lou. I'd told Phil I was staying in a swishy hotel, in the lap of luxury, and that's how it felt for the moment. I'd never lied to him before. Okay, maybe the odd fib – I wasn't a saint – but nothing on that scale. Right at this moment, I couldn't have felt less guilty.

At seven on the dot, dressed in a cute little denim romper and green T-shirt that matched the colour of my eyes, I entered the kitchen, fully refreshed. Alex was already there and just about ready to serve dinner. He turned and studied me admiringly.

'Wow. Look at you. New threads, I see.'

'New-ish,' I said, taking a seat at the wooden table.

'You discovered the joys of TCFCTSI then?'

I laughed at the recent memory. 'Boy, did I ever.'

'Geoff on good form, was he?'

'They make quite the double act, him and Auntie Lou.'

Alex gave the pan a shake and tipped out some more of those little Italian dumplings I remembered from before.

'I had some ingredients left over,' Alex said. 'So I've rustled up a new batch. I thought you might like to try them.'

'I told you,' I said, 'there's no need to go to so much trouble.'

Alex ladled a rich tomato sauce on top of the gnocchi.

'I love doing this,' he said, 'cooking for friends.' I beamed; we were friends now then.

'Every so often I have everyone over to the cottage and lay a big spread on.'

'I bet that makes you popular.'

Alex grinned. 'More popular than usual, that's for sure.'

Approaching the table, he set down two bowls of the most delicious perfect, plump and golden-brown gnocchi, smothered in home-made tomato sauce, basil leaves and toasted pine nuts.

'Here you go, tuck in. There's a dish of Parmesan right there next to you.'

Surveying the feast, I shook my head in wonder.

'I thought these things were supposed to put you off your food—upset, misery, heartache. Personally, I seem to be going in the opposite direction. If I keep on at this rate, I'll be round as a blimp.'

'Hardly,' Alex said, 'anyway, let's get back to the misery and heartache part. What lurks behind this woman of mystery? I think it's time you filled me in.'

Woman of mystery! I almost choked on my gnocchi. One popped out of my mouth and down my new top. 'Oops,' I said, rooting around my cleavage. 'Gotcha.' I considered the rebel piece of gnocchi for a moment and then stuck it back into my mouth.

'Um, you might want to clean up a little bit,' Alex said, gesturing in the general direction of my cleavage with a paper napkin. I took it primly and dabbed at myself.

Watching me do this, Alex burst out laughing, which set me off as well. Whatever air of mystery I'd managed to cultivate, there was sod all of it left.

Quietening down finally, Alex assumed a more thoughtful expression. 'Seriously though, Daisy, what are you doing here? What is it you're running from?'

I dabbed my mouth with the napkin, buying myself time, wondering how much of this I should share with a relative stranger.

'A troubled relationship,' I told him.

'Ah. Yes. That would do it,' Alex said.

I nodded, swallowing hard.

'Well, the worst is over at least. Although I'm sure it doesn't feel that way right now. At least you've managed a clean break.'

I shook my head. 'Actually, it's just on hold for now. We're going to try to work things out at the end of the month.'

'Oh. Right. I see.' Did I see a flicker of disappointment cross Alex's face? If so, it was gone the next moment.

'So why the time-out, Daisy, if you don't mind me asking?'

I blew out a deep breath as the reasons why came flooding back.

Alex held his hands up apologetically. 'It's okay. You don't have to tell me. I've pried enough already.'

I slumped in my seat.

'I caught him with someone else.' There, I'd said it.

'And this was yesterday?'

I nodded.

'Daisy, that's awful.'

'At least you have a better idea why I was acting so…loony tunes.'

Alex speared a few gnocchi with his fork and chewed them thoughtfully. Then he looked up from his plate. 'And you've decided to give him a second chance after catching him in the act?'

'Well, not in *THE* act,' I said. 'It wasn't going to go that far. Not according to Phil at least.'

'Phil being the cheating boyfriend?' said Alex.

He looked a bit sceptical, which annoyed me for some reason, and I found myself defending Phil's version of events.

'Well, Frannie did throw herself at him. That part I don't find hard to believe. I really wouldn't put it past her.'

I was on the defensive now, although I wasn't sure who I was defending or why. 'You don't know her, or Phil either, so really you're not in any position to judge.'

Alex shrugged, unconvinced. 'I guess you're right.'

'It's complicated,' I said, 'like any relationship.'

He nodded. 'True enough.'

'So, are you seeing anyone?' I asked, wanting to turn the tables on him.

'Me? No. I'm footloose and fancy-free.' It didn't sound like all that much fun the way Alex said it.

'Good for you,' I replied.

Alex gestured at my bowl. 'More?'

'What?' I asked, thrown by the change in direction.

Taking my 'what?' for a yes, Alex strode over to the stove, fetched the pan and ladled two dozen more gnocchi into my dish.

'What are you trying to do?' I said. 'I won't be able to make it up the stairs at this rate. I'll have to sleep downstairs in the bookshop.

'There's a name for what you're doing, you know,' I went on petulantly, the effect somewhat marred by the mouthful of food I was stuffing into my face.

'You're a Feeder!'

Alex laughed and held his hands up in surrender. 'You got me' he said, 'but curves—hell, I'm all for em.'

I laughed, but I felt better about tucking into the second helping. I normally had to make up excuses for a carb-fest or indulge in secret. It felt quite nice to have a partner in crime.

'So tomorrow,' I said, 'is there anything I should know about the bookshop before you throw me in at the deep end?'

'No need to worry. I asked Janice to come in. She can show you the ropes.'

'Oh. Right. You won't be around yourself?'

Alex shook his head, looking a little troubled. 'I've got a few things to do tomorrow. I'll have to close the café in the morning.'

'Joe can't run it alone?'

'He's up at uni for the day.'

There was a slight silence then, not exactly awkward, but I did feel the need to fill it. Getting to my feet, stuffed with gnocchi, I started clearing the plates away.

'What are you doing?' Alex said.

'Err, the washing up.'

'I'll do that,' he protested.

'You will not. You cooked, I clean. That's the rule.'

Alex, it turned out, had a stubborn streak as wide as his generous one. In the end we compromised.

Working in companionable silence, I washed, handing the soapy dishes over to Alex, who dried and popped them away. We stood close together, our fingers occasionally brushing. It felt intimate, like we were a couple. I tried to ignore the stab of desire I felt as he moved carefully around me.

Once we'd finished, we had nothing left to occupy our hands. We stood looking at each other, and I couldn't think of a damned thing to say. The atmosphere in the kitchen had suddenly become charged. His eyes dropped to my mouth and then dragged back up again.

I laughed nervously and took a step back, half expecting him to close the space between us and sweep me up into a kiss. I couldn't let that happen. Though just then, as he looked at me like that, I couldn't for the life of me remember why.

The moment stretched out becoming awkward until finally Alex said, 'Well, I'll be off then,' a slight smile on his face. 'I should get my beauty sleep. Some of us need more of it than you do.'

I smiled at the shameless flattery. To my surprise, Alex wrapped me up in a quick fierce hug. 'It'll be all right, Daisy,' he said, 'you'll see.' He pecked me on the cheek, said goodnight and then he was gone.

I made my way up to my room, suddenly exhausted. No Wolf tonight – he was at Alex's mum's – but I felt confident that I wasn't going to wake up crying in the dark.

I steered clear of Poe's gloomy tales before bedtime. On the way through the bookshop, I'd grabbed a copy of *Anne of Green Gables* and opted for a comfort read. After twenty-odd pages, I could feel my eyes drooping, so I switched off the light and hit the hay. But unlike the night before, sleep was hard to come by.

My mind drifted back to dinner with Alex. He was definitely flirting with me. I didn't imagine that, did I? And even more interestingly, why did the thought of Alex flirting make me feel suddenly breathless? *Oh no, Daisy, you bloody idiot.* I fancied Alex. *Well duh!* my subconscious said.

Well, it wasn't like it was going to go anywhere; I had enough on my plate already.

I felt an unreasonable flash of guilt. Was I in danger of throwing myself at the first man that showed me a little bit of kindness? That was a recipe for disaster. Maybe a fling would have been okay, a way to even the score with Phil—if I had the temperament for it.

But I knew myself too well. I knew I wouldn't be able to disengage my emotions. No, Alex and I were destined to be friends and nothing more.

I found myself thinking about Phil, our morning phone call and all its many implications. Apart from my little distraction at dinner, he had not been far from my mind all day.

I tried recalling exactly what I'd seen, comparing it with Phil's version of events. It lined up—sort of. But it could just as easily be bull. The only thing I could do was take him on trust. I would never have undeniable proof, so what else could I do but back him? If I loved Phil – which I still did – didn't that mean giving him the benefit of the doubt?

I didn't have the answers yet, but at least I had a full month to decide. Right now, a month seemed like a lifetime.

Nineteen

I was woken not long after dawn by the incessant crowing of Rodney the Bookshop Rooster. I'd managed to sleep through the unholy racket the morning before due to sheer exhaustion. Alex had told me about Rodney last night while we were washing up, so at least it wasn't too much of a shock.

The damned bird had impeccable timing, waking me up right at the, ahem, "interesting part" of an *extremely* smutty dream featuring Ryan Gosling. Another bird I wouldn't mind plucking.

Rodney then waited just long enough for me to drift off again before letting rip with a series of rusty squawks that drilled through my nerves like a jackhammer. I swear it sounded as though the little git was crouched on my pillow, crowing directly into my ear. This went on for some time while I lay staring at the back of my eyelids, grinding my teeth and trying to go back to sleep.

Ugh! I was never getting back to sleep. I threw the covers off, muttering about what I would like to do to Rodney with a stick of butter and a couple of onions.

I checked my watch. I wasn't needed for at least another couple of hours, when the bookshop opened. I wondered what to do until then. A little guiltily, I made for the bathroom and stood next to the empty tub. Although there'd been no mention of a water allowance, wasn't I pushing it a bit? This would be my third soak already. No, I decided. After all, I was being paid in kind instead of receiving a proper salary. Persuaded – rather easily, it had to be said – by this argument, I turned on the hot tap and picked a new essential oil to try. Mm, this one smelt like Christmas.

At half-eight, I made my way down to the main room of the bookshop. Janice was already behind the counter. At least, I guessed it was Janice. At any rate, an attractive woman in her early forties watched me with a welcoming smile as I ambled across the shop floor.

'You must be Daisy,' she said.

'Reporting for duty.'

Janice smiled at this. 'Right on time as well.'

As I came alongside the counter, she pushed a mug over to me. 'Here you go. I made you a brew.'

'Thanks. Just what I needed.' Then, to get off on the right foot, I made my apologies. 'I'm sorry if you got dragged in here today because of me.'

Janice waved it away. 'It's fine,' she said. 'I love the bookshop. I'm going to miss it when I leave Upper Finlay.'

'Alex said something about that.'

Janice nodded. 'My husband's job. It's taking us to the Gulf states. Given the pay rise, we could hardly say no.'

I nodded, taking a first sip of tea.

'Anyway,' she continued, 'I'm only in here two days a week now, with things being what they are.'

'Times are tough then?' I asked.

'Are they ever,' Janice said soberly. 'It's why I was a bit surprised when Alex told me he'd taken on someone new.'

'Ah well, you see I'm bartering my services for bed and gnocchi.'

Janice laughed. 'So I've heard. All very mysterious, I must say. Like something out of a Daphne du Maurier novel.'

'That's me—woman of mystery.' I was rather enjoying the label, inaccurate though it was.

'At first, I thought that maybe you and Alex were an item,' Janice added. 'That was my working theory, but then in this village I hardly see how he could have kept you a secret. Everyone knows everything around here.'

'No, I'm not his latest squeeze,' I said; then my curiosity got the better of me. 'Is that something that's happened before?'

Janice nodded. 'Back when Alex was still seeing Mandy, Trevor and Tina's girl, she used to help out in the shop sometimes. Although that was a hell of a long time ago.'

Hearing this, I was tempted to pry, wanting to learn more about Mandy and Alex's past. I made a heroic effort and reined myself in.

Janice smiled mischievously. 'So you'd have a clear run at him, if that was something you were minded to do.'

At this, I shook my head firmly. 'Oh no. It's nothing like that. It just seems a bit odd him being single, seeing as how he's so…'

I couldn't think of a good way to finish the sentence.

'So bloody hot?' said Janice.

'Is he? I really hadn't noticed.' This was such a bold-faced lie, that I couldn't keep a straight face. We both cracked up. I could already tell I was going to like Janice.

'The thing is I have a boyfriend,' I said. 'At least I think I do. Possibly even a fiancé.'

Janice frowned. 'That all sounds a bit vague.'

Looking to change the subject, not wanting to go over it again, I put my hand on top of the cash till.

'You'll have to show me how this thing works. It's been a while since my last job in retail.'

'It's easy,' she said. 'Not that there's much call for it. We're lucky to clock up a dozen sales a day.'

'Really?' I said. 'So few?'

'It's only the café that turns anything like a profit. Without it, Alex really would be screwed.'

'Then why close it this morning, do you think?'

'I guess he has his reasons,' Janice answered, looking away.

I got the impression she had a fair idea what these reasons were, but I didn't want to push it. Clearly, she was loyal to Alex and the bookshop and didn't want to say any more.

In the event, we clocked up eight sales that morning, which was pretty good going according to Janice.

'You must be a lucky charm,' she said.

I laughed, remembering how Alex had said something similar. To be honest, I thought most of those sales were from people who had popped in to have a nose at the new girl and then bought a random book to cover their tracks.

'Right,' she said. 'You can have your lunch break now. Take an hour. Take more than an hour. There's no great need to hurry back.'

'I'm thinking I should skip it,' I said. 'I've been piling the calories on ever since I got here.'

'That's up to you. But go and stretch your legs at least.'

'Funny you should say that; I was actually thinking about going for a jog,' I said. 'It seems like a good time to take it up again, with all these hills and dales on the doorstep.'

'Go for it,' Janice said. 'There're some great trails all around the village. I'd start with the footpath at the back of the bookshop if I was you.'

'I don't know,' I said. 'I've only worked one morning, and here I am skiving off in the middle of the day.'

'Go on,' said Janice. 'I'll soldier on without you.'

'Sure?'

'I'm bloody positive.'

'Okay then. I'll see you in a bit.'

Twenty

Upstairs, I changed into the frankly laughable running gear I'd picked up from TCFCTSI yesterday. For a sports-based charity shop, they hadn't had much apparel to choose from. The best I could manage consisted of a pair of *extremely* short shorts, an ancient T-shirt with Mickey Mouse on the front and a pair of bright neon trainers. At least I wouldn't have to worry about getting hit by a car.

'Right,' I said, brushing my hands together symbolically and talking in a falsely bright voice. 'Time to stop festering and moping. Daisy, old gal, you are going for a jog.'

I swept my hair back into a messy bun, made a half-hearted stab at some warm-up exercises and went downstairs, hoping not to bump into anyone in my outrageous get-up.

Sneaking out the back door, through the kitchen,

I followed Janice's directions and took a footpath that led off to the right, running parallel with the old canal. In only a few minutes I was scrambling over a stile and into a fallow field, surrounded on all sides by spectacular countryside. The fields were a patchwork of shimmering yellow and green. A tractor trundled happily in the distance, disturbing a flock of birds that burst up into the picture-perfect sky.

As I headed towards a forest, a few hundred yards ahead of me, I found myself reflecting on something Alex had said the previous night: *I'd better go and get my beauty sleep. Some of us need more of it than you.* I supposed he was just being friendly, but even so, it put a smile on my face.

Still, he'd suggested that I was attractive, even mysterious. This was not a commonly held view— that I had hidden depths; that there was more to Daisy Monroe than met the eye.

What Phil liked most about me, I think, was the fact I wasn't full of surprises. Compliant, I think would be the word. Ugh, is that who I wanted to be?

Anyway, I'd sprung a bloody great surprise on Phil this time, hadn't I? With that spiel about a job in Derbyshire and a stay at a luxury hotel. What a load of old cobblers and he'd swallowed it hook, line and sinker. I'd surprised *myself,* truth be told. But I rather liked this new side to my character. Daisy

Monroe, woman of mystery. Standing up to Phil, haggling with snooty shopkeepers. Flirting with hunky bookstore owners!

I was standing at the foot of a long, grassy slope, breathing heavily from my exertions. I put my hand on my knees. I had gotten pretty out of shape. Next to me, a soft whinny and a pretty velvet nose nudged my shoulder. I leapt back then laughed when I saw it was a chocolate-brown horse with large, expressive eyes. She was munching a mouthful of grass. I tentatively patted her nose as she leaned over the fence.

'Hello,' I said, distracted for a moment. I had never petted a horse before. And my hand was ready to be snatched back in case she bit.

After a while, she seemed to realise I had nothing for her. She blew a huff of air at me and trotted away. I suddenly realised that I could hear nothing at all other than birdsong and the faint hum of a tractor in the field opposite.

I decided to turn back for the bookshop, not wanting to take liberties, even though Janice had said it was okay. I'd only been gone a half-hour, but I still needed to shower and change my outfit.

Arriving at the back door, I pulled it open, expecting to pass through the kitchen unnoticed. Instead I ran into Alex. Literally ran into him. Flattening him against the wall in one fell swoop.

Stepping away, completely mortified, I saw that

I'd made a large sweaty mark on his T-shirt. I brought a hand up to my mouth.

'Alex. I'm so sorry. I didn't see you there,' I said.

Alex looked down at his T-shirt and then back up at me. 'I think you may have just ruined my look.'

'Oh, don't say that!'

A smile broke over his face, followed by the same infectious laugh I'd heard yesterday and the day before that.

'Come on, Daisy! I'm joking! Look at me, will you…'

He was in his scruffs—grey jogging bottoms and a tight, white T-shirt. His hair was sticking up at all angles like he had been raking his fingers through it. Bed hair. Oh boy.

Still, for all of that, I had him beaten in terms of dishevelment. A hot sweaty mess in a Disney themed T-shirt and a pair of too-short shorts.

'I've been for a run,' I said, stating the bleeding obvious. I tugged at the shorts feeling self-conscious about all the flesh that was currently on display. Alex didn't seem to mind. I rather suspected he was enjoying the view. 'I'm on my lunch break. Janice said that would be okay,' I said hurriedly, hoping he didn't think I was slacking off. 'I thought I better try to burn a few of those calories off.' I looked down at the shorts' stretchy elastic. 'I think I must have burned about three.'

'You look pretty good to me,' Alex said. 'Gorgeous. Smart. Funny. And a great dresser too!'

I swatted him. 'Ha, ha.'

'You're not one of those beautiful women who like to pretend they're actually quite plain, are you?' he said, rolling his eyes. There he went, flattering me again.

I snorted. 'Yeah right, that's me, Daisy Monroe, supermodel.'

Alex chuckled. 'Well, I think so.'

I blushed furiously. I mean I was fairly sure I wasn't repulsive. I was a bit of a late bloomer, truth be told. A (generous) description of me during my school days would be mousy. But Phil couldn't keep his hands off me at the beginning of our relationship and I always got a lot of attention when I was working at the pub. I guess I grew into my features, as they say. Even Mum said I had the nicest nose in the family. Whatever the hell that meant.

So why was I always so quick to put myself down? It was probably a self-defence mechanism. If I said it first, then no one else could hurt me with a cruel jibe or thoughtless comment. And to be fair, most of the time I was actually joking. Laughing at myself wasn't something I found hard to do.

Taking pity on me, Alex said, 'I've just made a pasta bake for lunch if you're interested.'

'Gah! You're a monster!'

'I'm a notorious feeder, remember?'

'Well…' I said, pretending to consider it when we all knew what the answer was going to be.

Twenty-One

Rodney was crowing particularly enthusiastically the next morning. I gave up trying to sleep and got grumpily out of bed.

I took a quick shower instead of a soak in the tub—I was still feeling a little guilty about using so much water. Then I made my way downstairs, thinking I might grab a cup of tea and sit in the garden for an hour. Maybe I would "accidently" sit on Rodney. I was unprepared for the chaos that greeted me in the kitchen. Alex and Joe were running around the place in something of a frenzy.

'Battle stations!' said Joe, skidding past me. 'All systems go!'

'A group booking for lunch,' said Alex over one shoulder, rolling out a length of dough. 'The Ladies' Guild. This was sprung on us late last night. The Carlyle let them down at the last minute. A small fire apparently. We'll be seating thirty, which is about ten more than we're equipped for, but what are you gonna do?'

'You should have given me a shout,' I said, moving towards them both. 'But I'm here now at least. Put me to work!'

'We had a load of new stock come into the bookshop yesterday. It's sad really, a widower selling his wife's collection of books. She died a few years back and he's moving into a care home.

'They need pricing up and cataloguing and putting out on the shelves. There are rather a lot of them; honestly, I shouldn't have taken them all. I think it'll end up costing me money. But well…would you mind sorting through them? I know it's early.'

'Of course not! And please call me if you need anything.'

'Okay,' Alex said, looking flustered.

I thought the best thing I could do was get out from under his feet, so I went into the bookshop as suggested and started poking through the newly arrived boxes.

By the time I'd finished, it was time to open up the shop. I'd barely turned the CLOSED sign around when the bell above the shop door rang and a sweet-looking little old lady ambled in. She had rosy crab-apple cheeks and a puff of cotton candy hair tucked under a plain mauve headscarf.

'Hello, dear,' she said, approaching the counter.

I straightened my back and smiled winningly. 'Good morning. What can I do for you today?'

'Yes well, I'm looking for a very particular book.' At this I nodded encouragingly and asked, quite reasonably, I thought, for the title. She considered this. 'Well, I expect it does have one,' she said, 'but I can't remember it for the life of me.'

'And the name of the author?' I asked hopefully.

She shook her head. 'No idea.'

'Hmm…' I said, pondering the matter, although frankly there wasn't much to ponder. 'Can you give me any more clues?'

'Of course, dear. It was about a donkey named Murphy. Oh, and it had a blue cover.' She paused to consider this, cocking her head to one side like a spry sparrow. 'Or possibly it was green, now that I think of it. Either way, I read it when I was just a girl,' she said dreamily. 'Oh, it was such a pretty book. Such beautiful illustrations.'

'Are you sure you can't remember what it was called?'

The woman looked at me sorrowfully. 'I thought you might know…'

'Erm, no. Not off hand. I could always look it up on the system, but I might need a few more details.'

The sorrowful look started to fade, replaced by

something more wrathful. 'That's not very good, is it?' she said forcefully.

'Sorry,' I said. 'I wish I could be of more help.'

She fixed me with a baleful stare. 'Call yourself a bookseller?'

'It's only my second day,' I said, put on the defensive.

But if I was hoping for sympathy or understanding, both were in precious short supply. Instead the old lady gave me another withering look. 'Just my fucking luck!' she said.

Despite her advanced years, she was sprightly enough to storm off in a huff and slam the door on the way out, muttering about unhelpful young ladies and inadequate stock. As the frame shuddered after her, I looked up at the ceiling.

'Great start, Daisy. Way to go.'

Putting it behind me, I started on my next job. Fortified by tea, I booted up the system as Janice had showed me yesterday and checked for online orders from Amazon. These would be packaged up and taken to the post office, ready to be mailed out with the evening post.

Thus began the frustrating task of trying to locate said orders from within the labyrinth of shelves. The task would have been far easier were it not for the perverse enjoyment the customers seemed to take in putting books back in the wrong place. I even found a copy of David Cameron's biography jauntily shelved under the erotica section. Each to their own, I guess.

Things picked up a little midmorning with several people browsing in the shop and I rang up a couple of sales.

The customers varied from charming to rude to sometimes downright peculiar. I'd quickly come to the conclusion that this was in part because a bookshop is one of the few places where you can legitimately loiter, making a pest of yourself for extended periods of time, without ever spending any money or being kicked out.

Later that morning, I spent an hour digging out a book for a gentleman in an alarmingly tight pair of cycling shorts, socks and sandals. Once we finally found it, he flicked through the pages enthusiastically.

'Oh yes,' he said, 'just what I was looking for.' He spent the next three hours cosily snuggled up in one of the armchairs reading it cover to cover. Then he put it back on the shelf and left without buying anything.

Later that afternoon, by which time I was up to twenty-three quid and a handful of shrapnel, the door was thrown open and in walked a couple wearing matching jumpers. They marched towards the counter with identically stern expressions plastered across their faces. *Uh oh*, I thought, reluctantly putting down my book—Ursula Le Guin's *The Word for World Is Forest*, which I had plucked from the shelves on a whim. Ten seconds after picking it up, I had been totally transported to the planet Athshe in that magical way that a good book can create a whole new reality for you.

I sighed, preparing myself to deal with whatever drama was about to play out in *this* reality. The vibe I was getting—nothing good.

They both came to the counter and made no reply to my hello, other than synchronised inclinations of the head.

'Can I help you?' I asked. After an uncomfortably long silence, the woman finally spoke. Her name was Tina, his name was Trevor. She had a thin, pinched face, deeply etched and mean. He had liver-coloured lips and couldn't keep his eyes off my tits.

'Nice to meet you,' I said, folding my arms across my chest. I was puzzled by their attitude. Had I offended them in some way? I couldn't see how as I had never spoken to either of them before.

Tina pursed her lips.

'You must be Alex's latest stray,' she said, leaning conspiratorially on the counter.

'Excuse me?' I said, thinking that I must have misheard her.

'Yes, we've heard all about you.'

'You have?' I wasn't particularly interested in

making conversation with this disagreeable pair, but this piqued my interest.

'I hear you're staying rent-free in the bookshop? And do you plan to stay long?' Tina asked, not giving me time to answer her previous question. 'Well, I suppose you would. Alex is quite a catch for a young lady like you.' My mouth dropped open. Where was this coming from?

'Now hang on just a minute,' I said as Tina's mouth opened, presumably to insult me some more. 'Are you suggesting that I'm some sort of gold digger?' I asked incredulously. *Alex owns a bloody bookstore that is barely scraping by*, I thought but didn't say it.

'Oh, no dear, of course not.' Trevor managed to drag his eyes away from my chest long enough to share a knowing glance with Tina.

'No need to be so sensitive. We're just looking out for Alex's best interests,' Trevor said.

'His father was a good friend of the family you see,' Tina said, 'and we wouldn't want anyone to, well…we're just looking out for him, that's all.'

Trevor nodded sagely. 'That's all, young lady, nothing nefarious.'

I was bright red by this point, steam coming out of my ears. *What would Ruby do in this situation?* Then thought better of it. She'd probably throw a book at Tina's head and end up in a jail cell. So instead I smiled icily and, channelling my inner Mum, made my way towards the door saying, 'Well, I thank you for your opinion.' I held open the door and waited.

'Now, now,' Trevor sputtered.

I continued to hold open the door.

Tina bristled. 'We're only trying to do what's best.'

'I'm sure you are,' I said. 'Now, off you pop.'

Once they'd left, I could hardly keep still behind the counter. Bristling with nervous energy, I decided to try to put it to good use. I thought about the little backroom office behind the counter where chaos reigned supreme. You could hardly move for the towering stacks of paper that had built up over the decades. The place was an ungodly mish-mash of old order forms, stray correspondence, and invoices from years ago. It had reached the point where Alex hardly dared stick his head around the door, let alone sort the mess out.

Given my long experience as an office temp, I thought I could perhaps be of use to him by making inroads into the confusion. Steeling myself for the chaos, I turned around, tried the handle, and opened the plywood door.

The door opened halfway and then got stuck, a thick sheaf of old printouts acting as a makeshift doorstop. I peered around the gap into the dim space, shocked by the scale of the epic clutter. Towering piles of A4, teetering stacks of ancient box files, and black plastic bags stuffed with more gluts of paper. Not only was Alex a feeder, it turned out he might also be a bit of a hoarder.

Taking a deep breath, I wedged myself into the crowded room as best I could and waded through the deluge. I thought the old desk might be a good place to start. At the very least, I could clear enough space so that you could see that a desk was actually there.

As I sorted the mountain of paper into orderly piles, I came across a stash of unopened letters that had been secreted away underneath it. They all looked pretty recent and I could see by the postmarks on the envelopes that some had arrived in the last month or two. A good two thirds of them were stamped URGENT in red. I gave a little shudder when I saw that. You didn't have to be Sherlock Holmes to guess at the concealed contents. I was looking at reminders from credit card companies, banks, utility firms, and the council, as well as debt agencies. Unless I was very much mistaken, what united this stash of letters was that they all related to debt.

I heard the tinkle of the bell as I stood there, wondering what to make of this discovery. Feeling troubled as well as guilty, I beat a hasty retreat.

Squeezing myself behind the counter again, I found a young man waiting on the other side. 'Well, hello there,' he said, resting confidently on the countertop, raising one eyebrow at me. He was cute in a jack the lad, here comes trouble sort of way. Under other circumstances, I might have humoured him a little, but now was not a good time.

'How can I help you?' I asked him flatly.

'Where to start…' he said, suggestively staring back at me.

After the little old lady, Tina and Trevor, and the unopened bills in the stockroom, my day's supply of patience was exhausted. 'Do you want a book or not?'

That did the trick. His inner Bond vanished. He removed his elbow from the countertop. Seeing I was in no mood to play Miss Moneypenny to his 007, he cut to the chase, digging deep in his trouser pocket before taking out a key.

'Would you give this to Alex for me? Tell him I owe him one.'

'And you are?'

'Liam,' he said. 'How's it going?'

'How do you think it's going, Liam?'

This time he looked at me in more of a thoughtful and less of a sexual way. 'I'd say not so good.'

'Well done. Clearly nothing gets past you.'

I was on a bit of a roll, sarcasm-wise. It was not unlike my phone call with Phil yesterday. It must have been a coping mechanism. I seemed to be channelling my inner Ruby, like I was standing in for my best friend while she was off on her travels.

Liam stared about him, not unsympathetically. 'It

would do my head in as well, working in here. I bet you have to deal with all kinds of nutters.'

This was the first thing he'd said that made me warm to him. 'Oh, you bet,' I said. 'Nutters of every size and description. Why only this morning I was confronted with nutters in matching jumpers no less.'

Now Liam grinned in recognition. 'You've met Tina and Trevor then?'

I nodded back at him. 'I had the pleasure about an hour ago.'

'Awful gossips the pair of them and proper nasty with it.'

I nodded again in full agreement. 'They seemed to think I was working here in order to weasel my way into Alex's affections and steal his vast fortune out from under him.'

'Ah well, I wouldn't pay them much mind if I was you. They're still sore that their daughter Mandy didn't steal it from under Alex when she still had half a chance.'

'Oh right,' I said. 'Anyway, I guess it's none of my business.'

'Isn't it?' Liam said, having a relapse, showing me more of his cheek.

I rolled my eyes at him, although the gesture was less harsh than before.

'Anyway,' he said. 'Thank Alex a million for me. If I hadn't been able to borrow his van while I got

my own heap fixed, I'd have missed out on one hell
of a job.'

'Okay. Will do.'

'Well, I guess I'll see you around then…'

'Daisy,' I said.

Liam raised his eyebrow again. 'How about I just
call you gorgeous?'

'Let's stick with Daisy, shall we!'

'Yes ma'am.' Liam beat a hasty retreat.

Twenty-Two

Leaving the counter bell as my able deputy, I went to give the key to Alex. I figured he'd be in the kitchen, chained to its hot stove, while Joe did the job of a dozen waiters out front in the café. Instead it was Joe I came across first, sitting at the table, looking absolutely shattered.

'Tough morning?' I said.

He lifted his head wearily. 'Absolutely brutal.'

'The Ladies' Guild put you through the wringer then?'

'You can say that again. Talk about exacting customers. Everything needed to be just so.'

'And was it just so?'

Joe nodded, although he was clearly too tired to take much satisfaction in the achievement. 'The food went down a storm. They praised it to the rafters.'

'And where's the chef? Is he out front milking the applause?'

Joe shook his head then nodded towards the kitchen door. 'No. He's out back in the garden.'

Following Joe's cue, I opened the back door and looked around, but I couldn't see Alex. I hadn't appreciated how big the back garden was, or how it had separate tiers leading downwards, but I guessed he must have been somewhere near the bottom end. Still holding the key in my hand, I drifted past mulchy beds overflowing with pretty, colourful flowers and spiky buds of lavender that filled the air with perfume. Neat rows of vegetables that would be picked fresh to go straight into the kitchen.

The chickens were out of the coop running free and I gave Rodney the side-eye as I passed. Lord of his domain, he seemed supremely unconcerned. Something of that lordly expression reminded me of Tina and Trevor and that unpleasant conversation drifted back to me. A stray, was I? "A girl like you!" What the hell was that supposed to mean? The more I dwelt on it, the angrier I got. They were the type of people who instinctively found a person's personal pain-point and pressed down on it hard with all the cruelty they could muster.

Finally, I spied Alex, shading his eyes against the sun as he put something to his lips and dragged on it furiously. Wolf was by his side, panting. Alex looked up as I approached.

In honour of my first solo day of work, I was wearing a cute yellow sundress—the pride of my charity shop picks. He shot a sly glance at my legs when he thought I wasn't looking. Little tip, we always notice.

'Liam asked me to bring you your keys,' I said, swirling my dress a little. I knew what I'd decided about me and Alex just being friends, but he looked so damned cute that I couldn't help myself. It was also a fuck you to Tina.

Alex cleared his throat.

'Thanks, Daisy,' he said, pocketing them. The way he said my name sent a shiver lightly across my skin. I immediately went crimson. Well, that served me right.

'You're a smoker then?' I said, trying to distract him from my flaming cheeks.

Alex stared down at the roll-up in his hand. 'Not normally. I still classify myself as an ex-one. It's only at moments of peak stress.'

'But you aced it. It couldn't have gone better.' I bounced up and down on my toes, excited for him. 'I hear the Ladies' Guild were all in raptures.'

Alex nodded soberly. 'It's true. They couldn't have been happier. "Ten marks out of ten."'

'Great, then they'll tell their friends, who'll tell their friends, and you'll be packed out every day.'

Alex nodded again, staring out over the garden, but he was lost in thought and looked painfully distracted.

'Maybe I should give you your space,' I said. 'You look like you could do with another minute or two.'

Alex turned, shaking his head, snapping out of his trance state. 'No,' he said. 'Stay here and have a beer with me. You're right, even a minor victory is worth celebrating.'

He flicked away the half-smoked cigarette, bent down and pulled out two ice-cold bottles, dimpled with condensation, from the cooler at his feet. Opening the first one, he handed it to me then cracked open the second. Tilting the bottle neck towards me, he offered a simple toast.

'Cheers, Daisy. Here's to you. Thanks for all your help. It really is appreciated.'

I hesitated before lifting my own bottle, although I could tell that Alex was being sincere.

'But I've hardly done anything,' I said, 'except stand behind that counter all morning and serve the odd customer. What I have to show for that, in real terms, is twenty-three pounds and thirty-six pence.'

Alex smiled at me with genuine affection. 'It helps you just being here, Daisy, if that doesn't sound too mad.'

I brought the bottle to my mouth, hoping to hide my flushing cheeks, and took a big slug of beer.

'Did you do all this?' I asked, gesturing at the garden, 'it's amazing.'

'Thanks,' he said. 'I like spending time out here when I can. It helps me to unwind. I call it gardening, but really it's just an excuse to drink beer in the sun.'

'Busted,' I said, smiling.

'Here, try this,' Alex said. He wandered over to a clutch of tomato plants loosely curled around vertical canes. He picked a particularly plump specimen and handed it to me. I ate it like an apple, sun-warmed and straight from the vine. Delicious.

'Is this basil?' I asked, looking at the green herbs that grew in profusion around the tomato plants. Alex pinched a few leaves from the stem and handed them to me. I rubbed them between my fingers releasing the scent and then stuck them in my mouth.

'Will you stay and chat for a while?' Alex said. I nodded and took another slug of beer. We strolled along the garden and sank into a rattan furniture set that was covered by a large white parasol.

Sitting in the shade with my legs in the sun, I idly ran my fingers through Wolf's fur while trying not to get distracted by wondering whether Alex was hiding another kind of six-pack under his T-shirt.

Wolf mooned up at me adoringly. I made a kissy noise at him. 'Good dog,' I said. His tail wagged enthusiastically. By now I was thoroughly in love with the old ham.

'So, I met Tina and Trevor,' I said apprehensively.

Alex snorted. 'You mean The Bitch and The Pervert.'

Nothing could have made me happier than to hear him describe them that way.

'They didn't seem too keen on me,' I said.

'What did they have to say for themselves exactly?'

I gave him the express version.

Alex shook his head in disgust. 'Unbelievable. At least it would be if I expected anything different from them.'

'She said she's a friend of the family?'

'On my dad's side,' Alex said. 'Their parents were friends. Dad and Tina used to play together as kids, and she seems to think that gives her some sort of right to poke her nose into our family's business. To be honest, I think Dad found her quite tiresome.

'Um…I used to date their daughter, Mandy too,' he said looking at me sidelong as though checking to see if that bothered me. I arranged my face into a neutral expression.

'I tolerate them both when it's necessary, but I won't have them upsetting you. I'll talk to them,' Alex said. 'Put them straight.'

'No, no,' I said, waving it off. 'No need. It's just, I guess, are people really talking about me?'

'Of course,' Alex said. 'Some hot girl arrives from out of nowhere and moves into the local bookshop.

I bet half the mothers in town have got you lined up for their sons. The other half are no doubt considering calling Interpol.'

'I hope to God you're exaggerating.'

'Well, maybe a bit.'

We moved on to talking about my favourite subject. Food! 'Well,' Alex said, when I asked him where he got his cooking skills from, 'my mum and my nonna taught me to cook. Then, of course, Joe had to be involved. When we were kids, Joe wanted to copy everything I did. Not so much anymore. It's good that Joe's his own man, but a little bit of hero worship wouldn't go amiss. I think he thinks I'm a bit of a hopeless case.'

I doubted anyone would think that, but I didn't say anything.

'Did you add the café recently?'

'A few years back. I thought it would help bring some extra revenue in.'

Something in his tone made me think he wasn't generating enough of it. That in turn reminded me of the hoard of unopened bills in the stock room. I saw them again in my mind's eye—that trove of troubling correspondence that Alex had sought to hide away.

'Did you buy the bookshop yourself?' I asked him.

Alex looked back at me and shook his head. 'No. It was Dad's dream. He's the one who started this place, built it up from nothing. Saw it as a civic duty as much as anything, with Upper Finlay having no library. When he passed away, there was talk of selling the place, although that's not what any of us wanted. Instead, I moved back here and decided to give it a go.'

As he spoke, Alex frowned as if he doubted the wisdom of following in his father's footsteps. I felt a sudden urge to kiss the line that appeared in his forehead. To sooth it away with my hand. I squeezed my fingers into a tight ball before I did something stupid.

'I miss Dad, we all do. It's like there's this permanent hole in our family where he used to be. But I've been really happy running this place these last few years. Being my own boss. I just wish it made a little more money.'

Alex was obviously in a deep hole, financially speaking. And it was going to take more than an occasional booking from the local Ladies' Guild to dig him out of it. Normally, he was upbeat and cheerful, but at that moment he appeared to have the weight of the world on his shoulders. As with the worry lines on Alex's forehead, I wanted nothing more than to ease the burden and make them go away. But what could I do? I was practically penniless myself. Suddenly, an idea came to me. There was one skill I had to offer.

'You don't have a website, do you?'

'You mean for the bookshop?' Alex replied. 'No. There's nothing very digital about this place.'

'Is that like a principled thing or is it because you're not sure how to go about it?'

Alex considered the question thoughtfully. 'Probably a bit of both.'

I shook my head. 'For all your practical skills, you really are a bit of a Luddite. You're not even on Facebook!'

Alex raised an eyebrow. 'Been checking up on me, have you?'

'That's not the point,' I said primly. 'I told you how I wanted to work in the digital industry, but I wasn't qualified and no one will hire me. Well, how do you fancy being my first client? What say I build you a shiny new website? I'm not saying it will transform your fortunes overnight, but it can't hurt, right? You've got this beautiful bookshop, amazing food…' *A hot proprietor*, I thought but didn't say. 'Unless they stumble on it by accident, no one outside of Upper Finlay even knows about it.

'I could get you set up with a basic online presence, a place where punters all over the world can find you. Not just the ones at the end of the street. Maybe nothing will come of it but we could at least give it a shot!'

I'd hoped my offer might have shifted Alex's worried look, but the creases remained on his forehead.

'That all sounds great, Daisy, but things really are a bit tight this month. I don't see how I could pay you.'

'Don't worry,' I hurried on, 'I wouldn't expect you to pay me. One thing I realised that's holding me back, it's like a vicious cycle. You can't get work in this industry without experience, but you can't get experience because no one will hire you without it! What I mean is, I can use you as a showcase of what I can do. And then there's your personal testimony, if you were happy with the website. A rave review wouldn't go amiss! Maybe it'll be enough to get me a job somewhere, even if I have to start at the bottom of the pile. Anyway, I don't want to get rusty, this'll help keep my skills sharp.'

Alex stroked his chin, not entirely convinced. 'I don't know,' he said. 'I'm not sure I'd feel comfortable taking advantage of you like that.'

'You taking advantage of me! That's a good one! You've done so much for me already, Alex,' I said, 'I feel like I owe you.'

He shook his head firmly. 'You don't *owe* me anything, Daisy,' he said. Oh dammit, I'd insulted him.

I put my beer bottle down by the side of the chair. 'Well, we can either spend forever arguing about who owes what to who, or you can let me get on with this.'

Alex considered it a little longer, his frown still on show. But finally it scattered and a broad smile replaced it. 'Okay, you're on, if it means helping you out with the job hunt let's go for it. Just as long as you're not expecting me to oversee this shiny new website in any way.'

I laughed. 'You're not getting off that easy. We'll make a digital native of you yet.'

Alex chuckled in response and sprang out of his chair, back to his usual upbeat self. 'Well, I'd better head in and see how Joe's getting on.'

When we returned to the kitchen, Joe was just ending a phone call. He took the phone from his ear.

'Making arrangements for tonight?' Alex asked.

Joe nodded. 'I'm meeting Annie over at The Blacksmith's for a few drinks.'

'Anyone else from your crew going?' Alex asked.

Joe shrugged. 'Mandeep said he might. Maybe Jack,' he said a bit grumpily. I had the feeling both Joe and Jack had their eye on Annie.

'What about you?'

'The Nelson,' Alex said.

'It's disco night at The Nelson Arms,' Alex explained to me, 'which is about as classy as it sounds. But by that stage nobody really cares. You're welcome to join us.'

Instinctively, I shook my head. 'I better not.'

'Oh, go on, Daisy,' said Joe. 'What's the point of spending time in Upper Finlay without sampling its world-class nightlife?'

I bit my bottom lip, undecided. 'Will there be many people there?'

'A few,' Alex said, 'but my friends are lovely and they're dying to meet you.'

'Alex has already filled them in,' Joe said, smirking.

'Well, maybe just for a bit,' I said.

'Are you saying you'll come?' Alex asked.

'Yes,' I said, 'I think I am.'

'Way to go, Daisy!' Joe offered me a high-five. 'We'll make a local out of you yet.'

'It's a miracle,' Alex said. I folded my arms and pretended to be cross.

'What time are we leaving?'

'I'm going to pop home and have a shower,' Alex told me. 'I'll pick you up in half an hour?'

'Oh God,' I said. 'I need to put some makeup on.'

'Good idea,' Joe said—to the amusement of all.

Twenty-Three

I hurried upstairs to get myself ready for the big night out, nervous and excited about what lay ahead. It may only have been a disco night in the local pub, but it felt good to put myself out there.

I felt a flutter of excitement as I checked myself out in the bathroom mirror. My hair was in its natural unruly state, but I found I no longer minded. Why, I wondered, had I been torturing my poor hair for all these years? It wanted to curl. So I should let it! I kept on the pretty sundress – nothing to do with Alex admiring it of course – and paired it with a cute pair of strappy wedges I'd found in TCFCTSI. *Not bad, Daisy. Not bad.*

I realised my elation also had to do with my offer to build a website for Alex. My head was already buzzing with ideas. As usual I was twenty steps ahead of reality, imagining a vast digital empire. Me at the helm—a female, British, slightly less wankery Zuckerberg.

'Nothing less than world domination will do,' I said, striking a pose.

But fantasy aside, could I really do this—build something that Alex could be proud of? Maybe help myself in the process? The little devil on my shoulder said, 'Of course not, dummy. You're living in someone's attic. You don't even have a proper computer.' I took a deep breath and brushed that devil away. I was tired of listening to her. From now on, I was going to listen to myself.

Well then, I asked myself, *Daisy, do you have all the skills you need to do this?*

I do, I replied. What, then, was I dithering for? I could give up. Wait for someone else to give me an opportunity to prove myself. Or I could give myself permission to try. *If you want to succeed*, I realised, *Daisy, you're going to have to do it your own damn self!*

I was so excited that I jumped up on the bed and did a little dance. Puffing, I sank cross-legged onto the bed. I was really going to do this.

Buoyed up by my pep talk and brimming with positivity, I bounced downstairs and graciously let Alex feed me home-made lasagne. As I helped myself to a second portion, I reasoned it was important to line my stomach if I was going to be drinking.

After that, we left by the back door and took a

route that was new to me. We strolled down a few narrow winding lanes that I hadn't come across before.

At the end of the last alleyway, The Nelson reared into view. Alex opened the door and we stepped through into the main bar of a proper British pub. Rough-hewn wooden floors and heavy oak beams. At the back, a long, wooden bar lined with chatting locals. I was immediately enveloped in an atmosphere of beery warmth and laughter.

'Well, this is the local,' Alex said. The place was buzzing.

'It's busy!'

'Just follow me.' He grabbed hold of my hand and I let him pull me through the crowded pub lounge. I was surprised by how many people I recognised, and we stopped and said hello to several of our regular customers; a group of now-tipsy tourists who had spent several hours browsing the bookshop that afternoon; and Janice and her husband, who were polishing off homemade steak pie and chips. A scruffy looking dog lay curled happily at their feet.

Tina and Trevor were in the corner with their daughter. On spotting us, all three pulled a face like they were sucking on a lemon. Alex gave them a curt nod and we moved on.

We spotted Liam, leaning casually against the bar, sipping a pint and chatting to the barmaid. He waved across at us.

'Your lot are outside in the beer garden,' he said to Alex.

'Cheers, mate.'

'Alright, Daisy love.' Liam gave me a wink. 'Looking good,' he said. I blushed.

For a moment Alex's grip on my hand tightened. Was he jealous? Liam was grinning knowingly.

'Come on,' Alex said, 'let's go find the others.'

'Sure.'

We stepped outside into the warm evening. The beer garden was dotted with groups of people sitting on wooden benches. Flocks of children ran around, squealing merrily, while their parents tried to round them up.

Alex stood for a moment craning his neck. I stood behind him, a prickle of anxiety in my chest. I felt suddenly shy. What if they didn't like me? What if I couldn't think of anything to say?

'There they are,' he said, pointing to a wooden bench full of people talking, laughing and drinking.

I plastered a friendly grin on my face then took it down a notch when Alex said, 'No need to be nervous.' He touched my arm lightly. 'It'll be fine.'

'I'm not nervous,' I lied. Alex laughed and wrapped his arm around my shoulders.

'Come on,' he said. I took a deep breath. *Here goes nothing.*

As we approached, there was a chorus of friendly

hellos and lots of hugs and backslapping until Alex managed to untangle himself and introduce me, going through the group one by one.

'This is Noah,' Alex said. Noah was a big, burly guy with a beard and a mop of messy hair.

'Nice to meet you,' he said, jumping up and wrapping me in a quick friendly bear hug.

'Oh,' I said, a little taken aback but pleased. 'Nice to meet you too.'

'This is Max.' Max, who was quite unreasonably handsome, gave me a casual salute.

'Man of few words?' I asked.

'Yup,' Max said.

'Never mind him,' Noah said, 'he's in one of his moods.' Max rolled his eyes and carried on drinking.

Alex moved on to a man and woman with dark hair who shared a striking similarity.

'These are the twins, Rosie and Jim.' I avoided making the obvious comparison to the classic children's TV show about the ragdolls Rosie and Jim. Instead I just nodded and said, 'Hi.'

'It's okay, you can say it,' Jim said. 'Our parents think they're funny.'

'Well,' Rosie said, tucking her arm around Alex's waist. She looked tiny next to his broad frame. 'We were starting to think you'd made her up.' Alex grinned down at her good-naturedly.

'I wish I was making *you* up,' he said.

'Get bent.'

'Hey, what about me?'

'Ah yes, saving the best for last, this is Cecilia—Cece.' Cece got languorously to her feet. She looked like one of those effortlessly cool girls. Not chilly, peroxided perfection like Phil's female friends. More like she'd cut her own hair with a bowl and some garden shears, fallen over into a pile of laundry and somehow emerged looking like a French supermodel. *Oh God, here we go,* I thought, determined not to be intimidated. Cece, it turned out, was also a hugger.

'Daisy, it's so nice to finally meet you,' she squealed, literally crawling over the table while the others grabbed at the half-full glasses lining it with a chorus of good-natured yells. She slid in beside me, wrapping me in a hug that smelt of jasmine and faintly of menthol cigarettes.

'Um, you too,' I said, from under her armpit.

After a while I tried to disentangle myself, as it seemed Cece had started a conversation and forgotten I was there. As I finally managed to wriggle free, Rosie slid into the seat on the other side of me and rolled her eyes. 'Honestly Cece. Put her down.'

Alex was still standing chatting to Jim about getting the next round of drinks in, which they seemed to be making overly complicated. In the end Jim said to me, 'Do you like wine?'

'Oh yes,' I said.

'What kind?'

'Um, white?'

Jim cracked up. 'You're going to fit in just fine.'

Twenty-Four

'How do you all know each other?' I asked the girls.

'Well,' Rosie said, 'obviously I'm stuck with Jim. We went to school with Alex and Noah and Noah works with Max.'

'Noah and Rosie used to date,' Cece said, leaning in conspiratorially.

'Really, what happened?'

'Oh you know, we were young. Nothing major, it just didn't work out. We're still really good friends though.'

'Unfortunately, her taste in men has got considerably worse since then,' Cece said.

'Anyway,' Rosie said, giving her the stink eye, 'Cece and I met years back at college. I was doing beauty therapy and she was taking photography. I ended up doing the hair and makeup on a shoot for the photography school and we hit it off. I'm a trained makeup artist now,' she said proudly, which made sense as her makeup was flawless.

'Do you still do photography?' I asked Cece.

'Well, I make a living from it,' Cece said. 'Mostly weddings, functions that sort of thing. I'd maybe like to branch out into something more editorial one day.'

'You will,' Rosie said, patting her hand. 'She's very talented.'

Jim came back with a bottle of Chardonnay. He plonked it and an extra glass in the middle of the bench.

'Thought I might as well get a bottle.'

'Cheers, Jimbo,' Rosie said, sloshing wine into her and Cece's half-full glasses and filling mine.

Alex glanced at me, smiling. 'You okay?' he mouthed. I nodded, beaming back at him. This was turning out to be fun. Alex slid down further along the bench, throwing glances my way every so often to make sure I was still all right.

Actually, I was. Generally, when I met new people, I could be a little closed off. I had a habit of deflecting questions back to the other person if I felt uncomfortable in a conversation. Rosie the master inquisitor, however, had prised out my entire life story – hopes, dreams and failures – before I'd hit the bottom of my first glass of wine.

On learning about my ideas for the website, Cece immediately offered to take pictures for it. Rosie jumped in, offering to do hair and makeup, looking pointedly at Alex whose hair was standing up in distracted spikes.

'*What?*' Alex said.

'The girls are just talking about doing your makeup,' Jim said, smirking.

'I don't know what you're laughing at,' Alex said to Jim. 'Don't think I've forgotten who she used to practice on when we were kids.'

'And bloody good I looked too!'

By the second glass, we were all gabbing away like lifelong friends. I couldn't believe they had accepted me so readily. More than that, they seemed to genuinely like me, even though I'd been a little reserved at first.

I'd already been invited to girls' Sunday brunch, where I would meet the rest of the girl gang, and also to Noah's birthday.

'Don't you need to check with Noah?'

'Huh?' Cece said. 'What's he got to do with anything?'

Rosie cracked up. 'It'll be fine,' she said. 'It's just drinks.'

'Speaking of which, the same again?' Noah rose to get the next round.

As we all nodded, then watched him go, Rosie leaned in. 'Anyway, more importantly. You and Alex, anything going on there?'

I spluttered into my wine. 'No, nothing like that,' I said.

'Yeah, yeah,' Rosie said, waving her hand dismissively. 'Tell it to the jury.'

'You can't ask her that,' Cece squealed.

'Why not? Someone needs to take that idiot off our hands.'

I laughed.

'Anyway,' Rosie continued, undeterred, 'you would make a lovely couple.'

'Whoa,' I said, putting my hands out. 'I'm not actually on the market, if you must know.'

'You're not seriously thinking about getting back together with Phil, are you?' said Cece. Then she put a hand over her mouth.

'Bloody hell!' I cried. 'No secrets with you lot, are there!'

Rosie shrugged. 'Sorry, Daisy. We're all big sharers here.'

I was pleased, even a little flattered, that they would consider me as a potential partner for their friend, but this was straying into awkward territory. I glanced over at Alex. Luckily, he was deep in conversation with the lads and didn't seem to have heard.

'It's complicated,' I said. 'Phil and I have been together for years. More than that, I still love him. It's not something you can turn on and off just like that, even after everything that's happened.'

'Poor Daisy…'

My default reaction was to be on alert for the hidden barb, but Rosie's face couldn't have been more sympathetic. Meanwhile, Cece had tucked her arm through mine and currently had her head resting on my shoulder, snuggled up to me like a giant, glamorous cat. Personal space, it seemed, was not her strong suit. I tried to relax.

'Anyway,' I said. 'I just hope Alex can put up with me for the next few weeks.'

Rosie rolled her eyes. 'Of course he can.'

'How can you tell though? I feel like he wouldn't say even if I was outstaying my welcome.'

'Well, for one thing,' Cece said, 'you're our friend now. Don't forget that.'

'That's right,' Rosie said, 'so who cares what he thinks?'

'Anyway, he obviously fancies the pants off of you,' Cece said loudly, slurring a little. 'I mean he literally can't take his eyes off you.'

She waved at Alex, who was looking over at us, alarmed. I blushed. Alex gave me a quizzical half-smile, turning back to Jim, who was deep in the throes of some sports-based anecdote.

'Keep your voice down, idiot.' Rosie elbowed Cece, causing her drink to slosh over the table.

'Bloody hell, Rosie,' Cece said, lighting a cigarette and waving it around dramatically. 'It's bloody obvious, isn't it? Doesn't mean anything has to happen, I'm just stating a fact.'

'What about you two?' I said, desperately trying to change the subject. 'Are you seeing anyone?'

'Oh God, don't ask,' Cece said, looking glum. In what just and fair universe these two wonderful women didn't have a harem of adoring men constantly prostrating themselves in front of them I didn't know. I guess the world is full of idiots.

'I always end up going home with that dickhead Liam,' Rosie said.

'Liam! Really?'

'Yup.'

'Then he never calls her, and she gets in a huff and ends up doing it all over again the next time he bats his baby blues,' said Cece.

'Oh, shut up, Cece,' Rosie said. 'Like your track record is any better.'

'Fair point,' Cece said.

'Do you really like Liam then?' I said, thinking, *That one's trouble, Rosie.*

Rosie shrugged. 'I must do. I keep going back for more and…' She leaned in. 'Honestly, mate, he's got the biggest—'

'Hello ladies, talking about me?' Rosie went beet red as Liam approached.

'You wish,' she said. Cece shook with suppressed laughter.

'Fancy a drink?' Liam said. Rosie folded her arms.

'No thanks.'

'Fair enough.' Liam winked at her. 'You know where I am.' He finished rolling a cigarette, licking it suggestively, and strolled off to join a group of lads.

'Oh my God, Rosie, he is such a bellend,' Jim said. 'Why the hell do you put up with it?'

'I know, dear brother, but he's just such a damn good shag.'

'Oh God,' Jim said, clapping his hands to the sides of his head. 'Too. Much. Information.'

'Teach you to mind your own business,' Rosie said sweetly.

Twenty-Five

As the sun dropped, it started to get a little chilly, so we moved inside as a group. All the chairs had been pulled back and the lights dimmed in readiness for the DJ, who soon began blasting out a medley of utter cheese.

The girls dragged me, protesting heavily, to the makeshift dance floor. I was a little stiff at first. But the others were just going for it, and my self-consciousness quickly vanished.

I had forgotten how much I liked to dance. I thought back to when Ruby and I used to have disco dance parties in her bedroom, dressed up as whichever pop stars we were obsessed with that week.

Recently, when I was out with Phil's friends, I'd started to feel like dancing was some sort of odd competitive sport. The men would all stand on the side-lines leering in while we stood in a circle, gyrating to some god-awful electronica, studiously avoiding eye contact with each other.

Now we were jumping and leaping all over the place, waggling about, looking like utter fools. Spinning each other around and then collapsing in gales of laughter.

The DJ kicked into an up-tempo Motown number and suddenly the dance floor was crammed. As Jim grabbed me and spun me around and Cece threw her arms around me, sloshing her drink, I realised I hadn't had this much fun in ages. My sides were aching with laughter and I felt overwhelmed with happiness.

The evening flew by and all too soon the lights flashed on briefly, signalling last orders. The DJ broke into a last-dance, smoochy slow number. Rosie was draped over Liam, whispering intently into his ear. *Dammit Rosie*, I thought. While I liked Liam, he was clearly a player. And Rosie was wonderful. She could do better.

Moody Max had left earlier in the evening, so now only Cece, Alex, Jim and I remained.

'My lady,' Jim said, bowing to Cece who jumped into his arms, pretending to smooch him while he backed away in pretend disgust.

'Just you and me then,' Alex said. He looked nervous, which was crazy. I swallowed. Oh boy. He put out his hand, and before I knew it I was leaning into him, his hand cupped around the curve of my waist, dancing tipsily.

He brushed my hair back from my face with his free hand and spoke into my ear so he could be heard over the music.

'Have you had fun?'

I nodded, not trusting myself to speak.

He spun me out and back again and I landed with my full body against his, my hands against his chest. I could feel his heart pumping beneath my palms. My hands slid up and around his neck. He pulled me in closer, his eyes half-closed. He smiled as we moved to the music, slow dancing, like teenagers at prom. He wasn't nervous anymore. He seemed to know exactly what he was doing.

I swallowed, biting at my lip, shivers running up and down my spine. Holy crap. I felt myself turn liquid and lean into him. I kept my head tucked down against his chest until he smoothed my hair back again from my face and hooked his finger under my chin, forcing me to look at him.

'Hey,' he said. In the dim light his eyes were dark, almost black.

'Hey,' I managed to croak back. This was getting embarrassing.

'You look so pretty tonight,' he said into my ear, his voice low pitched, raspy, sending more shivers lightly across my skin. I forgot to breathe. He was the only other person in the room. His eyes dragged down to my mouth so he didn't see the disappointment in my eyes when the overhead lights flickered and turned back on.

I hadn't even realised the music had stopped. Suddenly, we were just two people standing on a sticky pub floor, about to make out in full view of everyone. Someone shouted, 'Get a room.' *Good idea,* I thought as we awkwardly broke apart.

Rosie and Liam had left. Cece and Jim came over and said they were going to get chips. Alex and I were still standing close together. I couldn't think straight. I pushed him gently back. He looked sombre, serious.

'So…' Alex said, once we were alone again.

'So…' I answered. It hung on the air.

'Can I walk you home?' he asked. I nodded.

We walked in silence under a bright crescent moon. The night air was fresh, a breeze running cool fingers down my skin. Our shoulders brushed together. His fingers brushed against mine. I opened my mouth to say something, anything to break the tension, but nothing came out. Alex gently took my hand and wrapped his fingers around mine. His hands were calloused, rough from work. I tried not to think about them on my skin. Still neither of us had spoken.

I looked at him and caught him looking back at me. All too soon we were back at the bookshop.

'Well, this is me,' I said.

Alex smiled. 'Yep. This is you.'

He dropped my hand and brushed his fingers lightly against my cheek, lifting my face. Without thinking, I stepped into him. His eyes went dark, heated, and he walked me backwards into the doorway, out of sight of the street, until my back was pressed up against the wall.

His hands were shaking as they tangled in my hair. My arms slid around his neck as though they belonged there. Our eyes locked together. I couldn't remember the last time a man had looked at me like that. Maybe never. I swallowed, biting my lip.

'Can I kiss you?' Alex said, his voice deep with desire. 'It's all I can think about,' he whispered. 'You're driving me crazy.' He cupped my face, looking deep into my eyes.

My heart was hammering, my mind churning with indecision and lust. I felt short of breath. *I shouldn't be doing this. What about Phil?* And so stupidly, stupidly, I pushed him away.

'Alex, stop,' I said, my voice trembling.

He stopped instantly. His eyes were intense, his pupils dilated. He seemed to be struggling to breathe.

'What?' he said. 'Daisy, what's wrong?' I put my hands up to make some room between us. He stepped back.

'I thought...' He shook his head. 'I didn't mean

to…Oh God,' he said, looking mortified. 'I'm so sorry,' he said, backing away from me.

'No,' I said, 'you didn't do anything wrong. Please don't think that. It's my fault. I'm just…Alex, I can't do this.'

As soon as I said the words, I wished I could take them back. Alex looked like he wanted the earth to open up and swallow him whole. But my traitor's voice seemed stuck in my throat. The metallic taste of panic filled my mouth. I was so confused. I liked Alex. I *wanted* to kiss him. I wanted to do a whole lot more than kiss him.

Suddenly it was all too much, this inner tension. I turned and fled into the darkened bookshop.

Twenty-Six

That night, I cried myself to sleep. I was furious with myself. What had I been thinking? I'd ruined everything.

The next morning, I woke up early and sat on the edge of the bed. My head pounded and my mouth was dry. I gulped water from the tap, then splashed it on my face. I took a long, hard look at myself in the bathroom mirror.

I tried to examine my actions in the cold light of day, but my emotions felt slippery. Unreliable. Why had I let things go so far?

As I cleaned my teeth, I heard the sound of footsteps downstairs, quieter than usual as if Alex was treading on eggshells, trying not to wake me.

Oh God, I was going to have to go down and face him. Would he even want to talk to me?

Reluctantly I made my way down the stairs. Alex

was behind the counter, back-lit by the early morning sun that poured through the plate glass behind him. He looked tired, as though he'd slept badly. His strong jaw shadowed with stubble.

For a moment I just looked at him, my heart aching. Doubt crept in. I shook it off.

He looked up and when he saw me hovering, grinned sheepishly, running his hands through his hair. 'Things got pretty crazy last night, hey?'

I paused at the bottom of the stairs. 'I can leave if you want me to,' I said quietly. Alex regarded me silently for a moment, frowning.

'Come on,' he said beckoning to me, 'come over here.' I crossed the shop floor, my feet and heart dragging like lead.

'Why on earth would you think you need to leave, Daisy?' We were on opposite sides of the wooden counter. 'Hey,' he said gently, 'can you look at me?'

'Because of last night,' I said, lifting my eyes. For a moment I flashed back to his hands tangled in my hair. I felt my pupils dilate; a pink flush bloomed across my cheeks.

I opened my mouth, but nothing came out. He leaned in, looking at me. Holding my gaze while he waited for me to answer. When I didn't say anything he asked, 'Is that what you think about me, Daisy? That I would, what, throw my toys out of the pram because you didn't want to kiss me?'

'I led you on.'

He took my hand and I flinched. 'Sorry,' he said and dropped it, running his hands through his hair again.

'I, I can't lie. I like you. I think I've made that pretty clear. I'm just really sorry I put you in an awkward position last night.'

'No,' I said, 'it wasn't your fault. I should have been clearer with where I'm at.'

'We're adults, we flirted a bit,' he said. I blushed. 'But Daisy, this is not your fault. You can't make someone want to be with you if they don't. I hope you know I would never pressure you into anything. This is your home for as long as you want it. My pride's a little dented, but I'm a big boy, I'll get over it.

Unless...' He looked at me, his expression serious. Unless, what? I thought. *Unless what!* My cheeks flushed. His mouth curved upwards when he noticed. *Dammit, why does my every thought have to be scrawled across my face?*

'I'll take you as just a friend, Daisy. But if you ever change your mind,' he said lightly and shrugged. The bell rang, breaking the moment. I looked down, my mind whirling. Why was it so difficult to cut my feelings for Alex off? When I looked back up, he was chatting to a customer. The bell rang again and a gaggle of young mums with kids entered. The kids began to swarm over the shop.

One of the yummy mummies – an attractive twenty-something – stopped at the counter to ask Alex a question. She wound a piece of hair around one finger and snapped her gum. Looking at Alex as though she'd liked to spoon him up and eat him alive.

Feeling an unreasonable flash of jealousy, I turned away and busied myself sorting through a collection of books about the American Civil War. I had to stop this. Alex could talk to, and do, whatever he liked, with whoever he liked. I'd given him my answer. It wasn't fair to him to keep this up, nor was it right. I was probably going to be engaged in a couple of weeks. I'd never cheated on Phil and I didn't plan to start now. It would be the worst possible way to kick off our new beginning.

The woman purchased a postcard from the counter and Alex went around to hold the door open so she could manoeuvre the bulky buggy through. The baby gurgled at Alex and he knelt to chuck its cheek. Gad dammit, he looked like one of those men from the Athena posters in the nineties. Not fair!

The woman left with a swish and Alex came back over to me. Before, there would have been easy chatter between us. Now there was awkward silence. To fill it, I started to talk.

'Well, I've got a busy day ahead.'

'Oh? I thought you had the morning off?'

'The website,' I said. 'No time like the present. I want to get cracking.'

'Oh right. The website.' It had clearly slipped Alex's mind amidst all the drama, but I wasn't going to let that stop me.

'First things first, I'll need a laptop. You said Joe had one he could lend me?'

'Of course. I'll give him a call. I can have that here by mid-morning.'

'Excellent,' I nodded.

Alex nodded back. There was another protracted silence.

'So…I was thinking, if you don't mind, whenever it's quiet in the bookshop, I can work on the website. I'll have the laptop with me at the counter, so I can always switch between the two.'

'Sure, whatever you think.'

I was disappointed that Alex didn't seem more enthusiastic. He was probably still embarrassed about yesterday, so I didn't push it.

'I've got to take Wolf out for a walk,' he said, 'so I guess I'll see you later?'

'Okay,' I said glumly.

He smiled then, looking more like his usual self.

As he left that simple word from before – *unless* – hung tense and unanswered between us.

Twenty-Seven

Joe arrived at the bookshop around ten-thirty with a laptop tucked under one arm. He laid it on top of the counter.

'Here you go. I hope it'll do.'

'Looks good,' I said. 'What are the specs?'

'Specs?'

Clearly Joe wasn't any more computer literate than his brother.

'You know – memory size, processor, stuff like that.'

'It works with the internet,' Joe said helpfully.

I had to smile. 'Okay. That's something at least.'

Joe turned to leave, then he changed his mind. 'Do you know what's up with Alex today?'

I shook my head, attempting a puzzled look. 'No. Why?'

'I don't know, he seemed a little off when I spoke

to him earlier. I know you two have gotten pretty close. I just wondered if you knew what was bothering him. Alex isn't the best at talking about his problems. So sometimes we have to pry.'

'I'm sorry, I don't think I can help.'

Joe shrugged. 'I know you guys talk,' he said, 'that's a help in itself. I just...we're friends, too right?'

I nodded, realising it was true.

'I know you're leaving at the end of the month.'

'That's the plan.'

Joe ran a distracted hand through his hair in a way that was instantly familiar.

'I can see how you two look at each other. The way you look at him when you think no one notices.'

Oh boy.

'Just be careful with my brother's heart,' he said. 'Don't hurt him.'

'I won't,' I whispered, my eyes stinging. 'I promise.' Joe squeezed my hand.

'Alex is a great guy you know.'

I knew.

'Well, good luck with the website. I hope the laptop works out.'

I nodded, afraid my voice would crack if I tried to speak. He squeezed my hand again and left.

I didn't see Alex for the rest of the day. He was often on the road, driving out to look at book collections and private libraries to buy stock. But usually he would pop into the shop at some point, or be on the grounds somewhere fixing, moving or painting one thing or another. It felt like he was always on the go. He worked hard that was for sure. There was always some event, class or side hustle going on in one of the bookshop's many rooms. I swear I saw a group with Katana swords troop upstairs once. I thought it best not to ask, and I never saw them again.

My favourite days were the ones when Alex worked in the shop. We sometimes sat on the floor, surrounded by boxes and boxes of books, sorting through stock, chatting easily. Every so often his eyes would light up as he showed me a copy of something interesting or funny.

Even though he had said things were fine between us, I hoped his absence today didn't mean he was avoiding me. I missed him. Although I didn't miss the butterflies I got every time I entered a room, wondering if he would be in it. No. Those were involuntary, and unwanted.

After closing the shop, I slouched into the kitchen to fix myself something to eat. The space felt hollow and empty without Alex's presence. Thinking I could cobble together a sandwich or heat up some leftovers, I opened the fridge.

Inside was a pot of something gooey and delicious looking. A little card was attached with my name written on it. I turned the card over. *Tiramisu, your favourite x.*

I'd told Alex that in passing and had thought nothing more of it. I shook my head, feeling a bit tearful. 'Oh, Alex. What am I going to do about you?'

Twenty-Eight

Using Rodney as my alarm clock, I got up well before my shift in the bookshop started. I went for my morning run, showered, then booted up Joe's laptop.

Waking so early every morning – thanks to Rodney – gave me plenty of time to brood. And by brood, I mean of course, relentlessly checking Phil's status on Facebook.

I navigated to his page, annoyed with myself even as I did it. It was like a compulsion. Much as I wanted to be a strong, independent woman in the vein of Destiny's Child, apparently, I was not.

I scoured the page for any sign of Frannie. But she was conspicuously absent. This was a good sign; normally she was all over Phil's feed like a rash.

I glanced again at the most recent photo. In it, Phil was standing outside the gleaming windows of a high-end jewellers. He had one thumb up and was grinning ear-to-ear, like an extremely well-groomed Cheshire cat. Another picture showed a display case packed with stunning diamond rings.

The first comment was from Seb, Frannie's husband: *Something you want to tell us old chap?*

Underneath that, Phil had offered a winking emoticon and a highly suggestive comment: *Watch this space...*

My heart started beating wildly. When he'd spoken about us taking the next step, deep down I'd wondered if he was spinning me a line. Trying to limit the immediate damage. But it looked as though he was deadly serious, had maybe even gone ahead and bought the ring.

Okay, so perhaps it wasn't romantic in the traditional sense – him dropping hints on Facebook, but that was just his way. Phil was one of those, look how great my life is, I bet it's better than yours, type of people who needed to broadcast whatever he was up to for the whole world to admire. I'd lost count of the amount of retakes and filters it had taken over the years to achieve that effect.

And yet for all his faults, even his – maybe – infidelity, I missed Phil. I missed our life together. I was used to seeing him every morning when I woke. Used to the subtle routine you develop when you share a life with someone. In spite of myself, I was excited to think that our relationship was about to become a matter of record. There was no bigger statement you could make than marrying someone. It *proved* he loved me…right?

I looked at the time. Oh shoot, I'd meant to make a start on the website, but I'd wasted yet another morning fretting over bloody Phil.

Two hours into my shift and still no sign of Alex. I'd only had one visitor so far this morning: Terry, a gruff Yorkshire man, who'd been the landlord of the Nelson pub until he retired ten years ago. Now he created beautiful miniature oil paintings of the Derbyshire countryside, which Alex sold in the shop for a healthy profit.

I chatted with Terry for a while before he left me with three sublime renditions of the sweeping green hills of the Hope Valley.

Auntie Lou popped in later and we spent a happy hour hunting down a collection of Jackie Collins bonkbusters for her to consider. After an in-depth discussion, bordering on the academic, about which was the raunchiest, she decided to go with *The Stud*.

With all my jobs for the day done and no more customers on the horizon, I opened the laptop again, determined to make a proper start on Alex's website.

I took out my mock-up of how each page on the website would look. Then I created a plan of everything I needed to do and broke that down into manageable chunks. Once I had my plan fully formed, I opened up my text editor and started to code.

Before I knew it, I found myself in the zone, neat, elegant lines of code flowing from my brain to my fingertips, and then on into reality. My brain turning over solutions as quickly as I could type.

'What ya doing, Daisy – writing a novel?'

I jumped surprised to find Janice standing in front of me leaning over the counter. I stared at the bell above the door. 'Is that not working?'

'It's working fine,' Janice answered. 'You were off in la-la land, or wherever it was you just went.'

'Coding heaven,' I said, smiling at her.

'Right. Coding heaven.' Janice pulled a face, 'I think I'll stick to regular heaven.'

'I'm building a website for the bookshop,' I explained.

At this Janice nodded approvingly. 'Bloody brilliant,' she said. 'I told Alex yonks ago he needs to pull his finger out and bring this place up to date.'

'Well, hopefully this is a step in the right direction,' I said.

'So, you're a computer whizz? Hidden talents, I see.'

'Very hidden,' I said. 'Trust me.'

'Don't put yourself down, love. There's plenty of others who can do that for you.'

'That's for sure. Anyway, I didn't think you were in today,' I said.

'Boredom,' Janice said. 'Sheer bloody boredom. So I thought I'd pop in for a natter.'

'Natter away,' I said.

Janice nodded. 'Fancy a brew?'

'A cup of tea would be lovely, thanks Jan.'

A short while later, Janice returned from the kitchen with a steaming mug in either hand. 'You two had a tiff then, have you?' she said.

I tried acting the innocent. 'Which two?'

'You and Alex.'

'What makes you say that?'

Janice shrugged. 'I saw him in the village earlier. He went all coy when I asked him how you were. I've been around the block a time or two, Daisy love.'

This explained Janice popping in for a natter. She was fishing! I picked up my mug and took a sip, stalling for time. As I did so, Alex peered around the door, looking a little nervous.

'Speak of the devil,' said Janice.

'You were talking about me?' Alex looked alarmed.

'Only nice things,' Janice said, taking pity on him.

'Oh. Right. Okay.'

'So what can we do for you, boss?'

'Erm, I was hoping I might have a word with Daisy.'

Janice nodded on my behalf. 'I think that would be okay.'

Clearly, he wanted a private chat, but Janice remained welded to her chair. She might as well have been holding a bucket of popcorn.

Alex scowled at Janice. She dunked her biscuit in her cup of tea and gave it a good swirl.

'Spit it out, lad.'

'Um well, Daisy, actually I was wondering…Um, I've got a night off tonight. In the spirit of being friends and all that, I wondered if you wanted to pop over to mine for some dinner?'

Janice smirked.

Bad idea, I thought, being alone with Alex all evening. At night, drinking wine.

'That sounds fun,' I said brightly.

Twenty-Nine

Alex held open the door and I clambered into the front seat of his white van. Wolf sat beside me, his head hanging out the window, tongue lolling.

We drove down a winding country lane lined with hedgerows and ancient, crumbling dry-stone walls. All around us were high, densely wooded hills and craggy peaks. The road was dappled with pooling shadows in the gathering dusk, the air perfumed with flowers.

'It's so beautiful here,' I said.

'It sure is,' Alex said, glancing over at me. We locked eyes. There it was again, that crackle of electricity.

'Eyes on the road,' I gently chided, and dear God, Alex blushed. I felt a rush of goddess-like sexual power.

'Sorry,' Alex said, 'last time, I promise. Scouts honour.' He made the sign.

'Hands on the wheel!' I shouted and just like that we were laughing again.

'Well, here we are.'

Surrounded by rolling hills, the cottage was picture perfect. I laughed delightedly. 'Okay, now I see why you wanted to join the property owning classes.'

'You like it?'

'I really do.'

'Still needs plenty doing to it, of course. She's a bit of a fixer-upper. It helps that I can do most of the work myself.'

God, that was hot. I had trouble changing a lightbulb.

We crunched up the gravel path, Wolf bounding ahead of us. Alex unlocked the door and we stepped inside. Wow. The whole cottage was open plan with polished wooden floors and exposed oak beams stretching across the high ceilings. The modern kitchen had black granite tiles and an island counter. At the far end were sofas and a cosy looking living area.

There were still signs of ongoing work; one wall was half painted, with a protective tarp under it, and what looked like a gorgeous real brick fireplace was being slowly revealed from under ugly plaster. There were several large stacks of books and Xbox games on the floor and no shelves yet to house them.

'Well, this is home,' Alex said.

I drifted into the kitchen pulled by cinnamon strings. The cottage smelt divine.

'Have you been baking again?'

'I have. Want to lick the bowl?'

'Um…yes.' He held out the spoon. I took it and slid it in my mouth, suddenly overwhelmed by bittersweet dark chocolate. I closed my eyes.

'Oh my God, that's good,' I said, licking my lips. Alex cleared his throat.

'I thought it might be nice to eat outside,' he said. 'Maybe fire up the grill. I've got some steaks we could throw on. Maybe a nice glass of red to go with it.'

'Yes please,' I said.

He laughed. 'There's a couple of bottles over there in the rack. Choose one you like.'

Honestly, I couldn't tell the difference when it came to wine. I picked the one with the fanciest label.

'Good choice,' Alex said.

Alex turned to an old record player. He lifted the needle and set it in the groove. A pause and a song crackled into life.

'Vinyl?' I asked.

'It was my dad's. Another sign that I'm behind the times. To be honest, I used to try and impress girls with it at uni.'

'Did it work?'

'Nope.'

'Where did you go to university?'

'Durham,' he said. 'I majored in Engineering, then I moved back to Derby after and got a job at Rolls Royce.'

'Fancy,' I said.

'When Dad passed away, I came back to Upper Finlay and took over the bookshop.'

'That must have been a difficult decision.'

'Well, I was earning good money, but it wasn't exactly my calling in life.'

'And is that what the bookshop is to you?'

'I guess it is. I really do love it.' His forehead creased in a brief frown.

'And you, Daisy? Is that what coding is – your calling?'

I was a little taken aback. No-one had ever asked me that before, my boyfriend included. After giving it some thought, I nodded. 'To be honest, it took me by surprise,' I said, 'I never really expected I would be capable of something so…academic. I think that's why it felt like such a kick in the teeth when my boss decided I wasn't, I don't know, good enough. Educated enough.'

'But you didn't let it get you down. That's one of the things I admire about you. Your drive.'

I smiled, pleased with the compliment.

'Maybe you're best off out of there anyway. It doesn't sound like this Oliver valued you the way he should.'

'But I worry. I mean will anyone ever hire me again?'

'I've hired you! You're building me a super-fancy website. As soon as it's finished, I'm going to sing your praises to the high heavens and recommend you near and far.'

'Woah,' I said. 'Hold your horses. It might suck for all you know.'

Alex shook his head firmly. 'No way. I have complete faith in you. It's going to be great.'

'You're a shameless flatterer,' I said to him. 'You know that, right?'

'I'm a notorious feeder too, remember? Come on, let's get you fed.' Alex gently steered me outside, lightly touching my elbow, being careful not to overstep his bounds.

I sat on a little patio-set in the small but pretty garden, sipping the excellent wine I'd chosen, watching Alex work the grill. We chatted easily, the lingering awkwardness between us slowly fading. I was glad now that he had invited me.

'Here we go,' he said, setting a perfectly cooked steak down in front of me.

I helped myself to salad and another glass of wine. For a few minutes we were busy eating, comfortable again with silence. I found myself thinking about our friendship and just how much Alex had come to mean to me in such a short amount of time. Looking at Alex, I could sense he was less relaxed. He seemed troubled, a little on edge, although he was trying to hide it.

I was pretty sure things were okay between us again, but I knew something was wrong. I recalled the pile of unopened bills I'd found in the stock room. Perhaps his finances were worrying him.

I didn't have any great desire to bring it up, but I knew it needed addressing. I had to know just how bad things had gotten for him – wasn't that what friends were for?

I put my fork down and Alex looked over at me when he heard it clunk against the plate.

'The other day,' I said, trying to think of the best way to broach the subject. 'I thought I'd give the stock room a tidy. After what you said about it being a mess, I decided to make a few inroads into the chaos…'

Alex's shoulders slumped.

'And?'

'And while I was clearing the desk, I came across this big pile of unopened mail…'

'You saw that then?' Alex said.

I smiled in sympathy. 'I guess that means you did know they were there?'

'It's where I put them – the letters I don't dare open. Which in the last few months means all of them.'

'But that's…' I couldn't think how to finish the sentence.

'Madness,' said Alex. 'I know. I'm making a terrible situation even worse, although I doubt that's actually possible. Things are about as bad as they can get.

'I don't think anyone could have predicted the disruption independent booksellers were going to face starting in the nineties, but even so, first Dad and then me, we fought against the tide. We did everything we could think of to supplement the income from book sales. Book launches and signings, author readings and book groups of every description. I cooked up literary lunches, book curation services, we even tried children's story time and birthday parties. Renting out our rooms to anyone and everyone. But nothing was ever enough,' Alex said, visibly upset. 'It's been a slow slide, with things gradually getting worse and worse and I've had to borrow more and more just to keep our heads above water.'

'What are you going to do?'

'Lose the bookshop,' Alex said. 'At this stage, it's only a matter of when.'

'No!' I cried.

Alex allowed himself a weary smile. 'I don't think I've got any choice.'

I shook my head ferociously.

'No, Alex. Don't say that. There has to be a way.'

Alex stared down, poking at his food with his fork. 'To be honest, Daisy, I don't know what else I can do. I've remortgaged the house; I might lose that too.'

My mind raced into action, casting about for solutions. 'Couldn't your mum help you out? I know you might not want to ask her, but I'm sure she'd hate to see the bookshop leave the family.'

Alex shook his head vehemently. 'I couldn't.' He sighed. 'There was an…incident, last year.' He put his head in his hands. 'She fell for one of those telephone scams.'

'Oh no!'

'Apparently, it had been going on for months. It could have been a lot worse, in all honestly. But most of her savings are gone. The bank won't reimburse her even though they say they will in these cases. I can't even be cross with her. Honestly, when I heard the details, I can't say I wouldn't have fallen for it too.

'She doesn't even know about all this. If I lose the bookshop it'll be like losing another piece of Dad. I don't know how she'll cope with it. They had one of those marriages, you know, that just seem to work. They were always laughing. And then he was gone. A car accident.'

'Oh Alex, that's dreadful.'

We both took a large slug of wine.

'Does anyone else know? About your situation, I mean.'

'Joe knows some of it. Janice too. But the only ones to know the real extent are me and now you.'

'Okay, then,' I said. 'What *is* the real extent.'

Alex paused, winced, and took a deep breath. 'More than any amount of book, cake, or quiche sales is ever going to clear.'

'There has to be a way.'

Alex shrugged miserably. 'I don't see how.'

'No wonder you started smoking again,' I said taking another large glug of wine.

'You've helped,' he said. 'It's been better since you got here.'

I swatted the idea away. 'Me! What have I done?'

'Just having someone to talk to. I'm not the best at that. I tend to try and fix everything myself. Then it all builds up, you know?'

'What about Jim, Noah, Rosie and the rest of the gang? Can you talk to them? I'd say you're pretty blessed in the friend department.'

He nodded. 'You're right. I am pretty lucky there. But I just feel like…it's different with us.'

'Me too,' I said softly.

Our eyes locked. Alex didn't move a muscle, but I could see his pulse beating in his throat. My heart started pounding. I knew he wanted to kiss me again. I have never, in all my days alive on this planet, wanted to kiss someone more than I did right at that moment.

'I think I should go home now,' I croaked. Alex exhaled.

'My God, woman,' he said. 'You're going to be the death of me. Come on. I'll drive you home.'

Thirty

'Oh for goodness' sake, loosen up,' Cece said, grabbing me by the shoulders and shaking. 'Would it kill you to give me a hug!' I huffed, then hugged her anyway. It was inevitable. Might as well just go with it.

Cece had meant business when she said she would take professional photos for the website. Yesterday, she and I had gone for lunch, to, as Cece put it, conceptualise the shoot.

'So what do you want me to do?' she'd asked. Straightforward. No question in her mind that I had a clear vision. My impostor syndrome loosened its stranglehold another inch.

When I'd come down this morning Cece was already busy, snapping a series of generic shots. 'Just getting in the zone,' she'd said airily. Janice was behind the counter sipping tea. No sign of Alex.

Today Cece was wearing some kind of tie-dye

monstrosity, secured at the waist with what looked like the inside of a bicycle tire. Naturally, she looked fabulous. She was on highly excitable form bouncing all over the place and bossing everyone around.

I'd never done anything like this before but I'd prepared as best I could. And Cece was a great collaborator, refining my ideas until we had a solid concept and a list of specific shots we needed to check off. We decided that we wanted the images to show a friendly, community atmosphere. Quirky, authentic and natural with warm tones. We wanted customers to feel like part of the family.

Having met our customers I wasn't sure how I felt about that one. Luckily, this was for Alex, who was endlessly patient and charming with them. Not for a cynical old cow like myself.

We'd even managed to wrangle a few of the more compliant customers into joining the shoot. We were going to pose them in various, hopefully natural-looking scenes; browsing, reading and up in the restaurant eating some delicious concoctions Alex had come up with. We also had the usual litany of events – Book Club, gin tasting and open mic nights running throughout the week. Cece, bless her, planned to pop into these with her camera as well.

As I'd sipped mimosas over brunch with Cece and we drew up our plans, I'd realised with some amusement that I, Daisy Monroe, was on the verge of directing my own photoshoot. I might have been paying for it in prosecco and eggs benedict, but hell, it was a start. Who would have seen this coming a few weeks ago?

The bell above the door rang and Rosie came in on a blast of air with Joey trailing behind her. 'I found this one loitering on the street outside,' she said. Joey pooched out his lip.

'I was just chatting to some mates,' he said.

Cece clapped her hands. 'We're on a tight schedule, people. We don't want to lose the light.' The front of the shop had lots of natural light flooding in through the windows. Deeper in, it got a little murkier. Cece did have a lighting kit, which would help in the deepest, darkest corners of the bookshop. Waif though she was, she'd still somehow managed to lug the whole lot inside and set it up all by herself.

'I would have helped you with that,' I said.

'Ah thanks, chick,' she said, 'but I'm used to it.'

Rosie tucked her arm through mine. She had her professional bag with her; a neat black case, the strap slung over her shoulder. 'Right, where is he? I'm going to pin him down and physically force him to have his hair cut.'

'In the kitchen, I think.'

'So that just leaves you, Daisy,' Rosie said. 'I've been dying to get my hands on all that hair.' She made a scrunching gesture.

'It's not that bad is it?'

'No, it's bloody gorgeous, maybe that's why Alex fanci— Oops sorry, we're not meant to be talking about that are we?'

'Um,' I said, unsure what she knew.

Cece collapsed into giggles.

'Love you Rosie, but you're such a blabbermouth.'

'What! How am I supposed to keep up with what I'm not meant to say? If it's not those two dicking about then it's some other drama!' Rosie said, indignant. 'Anyway,' she carried on, 'I just want to take a little weight out of the back.' She was running her fingers through my hair. 'Shape it up around your face. And then with the makeup, I want to keep it quite neutral, but your eyes are such a pretty colour I think a bright lip would really make them pop.'

'Oh,' I said, 'okay.' Unsure but trusting Rosie. 'I hadn't realised I was going to be in the photos too.'

'Well you're staff, aren't you? We need you for the group shot.'

'Okay, fine,' I said reluctantly. Self-promotion – the horror!

Wolf, overexcited by all the commotion, was pawing at everyone and getting underfoot. He was photogenic though, mugging for the camera whenever Cece snapped a shot.

I hung back, chatting casually with Joey and watching Cece boss the customers about, posing them in various positions while Rosie chased them around with the lint roller. Cece, I noticed had a natural warmth to her that put people at ease, seeming to make them forget they were in front of the camera.

Half an hour later, as we were discussing the second half of the shoot, Alex and Rosie came down from upstairs. I nearly lost my breath. Holy Mother of Dragons, he looked good. Rosie had cut his thick, dark hair short. He was wearing his glasses. His jeans and polo fit him like a glove. I thought I might have to roll my tongue back into my mouth like a cartoon cat. Bloody hell, if we put him on the website looking like that we were going to be flooded with horny women…and men. Aliens, probably too.

Dark eyes looked my way. He looked serious for a beat, no trace of a smile. Then he grinned at me a little goofy, embarrassed at all the attention.

'Well?' he said, 'will I do?'

'Um yes, very nice,' I said stiffly. 'Good job Rosie.'

I heard Cece snort behind me and carried on talking, though lord only knows what I said. Determined to style it out, even though my heart felt like it was going to hammer its way out of my chest. Dammit. You could mentally decide that you didn't want to be with someone but there was no stopping a physical reaction.

Alex's eyes crinkled at the corners. Was he laughing at me? The corner of my mouth inched up.

'Right-oh,' Alex said smirking. Yup, he was teasing me. And suddenly I was giggling too, remembering our awkward behaviour the first night we'd met. When I'd almost dropped my bath towel and flashed him a sneak preview of the goodies. The others were shaking their heads, confused, wondering what the joke was. But they were laughing a little too. We finally managed to get a hold of ourselves and I attempted to carry on in a professional manner, rather than drooling over my client.

'Right,' Cece said an hour later. 'Have you got everything you need?' I quickly ran through the list and nodded. 'Okay then.' She clapped her hands together. 'That's a wrap.'

Thirty-One

In the following days, every time I saw Alex, whether in the kitchen, café, or bookshop, all I wanted to do was put my arms around him. Give him a hug and tell him everything was going to be okay. But I couldn't do that. Because, honestly, I wasn't sure that things would be.

Now I fully understood the mess he was in, I could hardly sleep for worrying about it, thinking about all the weight he had been carrying around, all by himself. He might lose the bookshop, his beautiful cottage that he'd worked so hard on. He was still grieving the loss of his father. His worries about his mum. Through it all, when a stranger had turned up on his doorstep, a bedraggled mess, he'd dropped everything to help me.

Although I continued work on the website with the same dedication as before my perception of the project had altered. I'd wanted it to be the answer to Alex's problems, but that was before I understood the depth of them. As for Alex I think he'd started to think of the website as a kind of memorial. Something to remember the bookshop by once it was gone.

When Cece came in to show us the photographs, Alex seemed melancholic while we reviewed them. Like he was already looking back on happier times. His fixation on the past saddened me. I'd wanted to equip the business for the 21st century, but he'd come to think of the website as a digital tribute to something that would soon be lost. Either way, I put my heart and soul into the design. If it was going to be a memorial, then I was going to make it the most beautiful and poignant version I could create.

By the following week, I had the hosting configured, the domain registered and had started to test the website across browsers and devices.

After countless hours consumed by the project I sat back in my chair and examined the work critically. It looked professional but friendly, warm and inviting, elevated to something special by Cece's beautiful photography. The tight, excited feeling in my belly told me it was good.

I made a final few adjustments and, heart in my mouth released the website into the wild. Pushing it live for all the world to see.

I didn't expect this to generate much, if anything,

in the way of visitors, but I wanted a "soft" launch first. That way it could be up and running for a few days, letting me iron out any last glitches before I showed it to Alex.

When I woke early the next morning and checked the analytics, I was expecting zero hits. To my surprise, thousands of people had already visited the website. *That can't be right,* I thought.

Digging deeper, I found that the flurry of visitors came from all over the planet. The US, South America, India, China, New Zealand, you name it. All of the search terms focused on some variation of the phrase "*tom benchley upper finlay*" and "*books*". Although there was no mention of anyone called Tom Benchley on the website, the dark magic of the internet had somehow managed to push us onto page two of the search engine results page. Weird.

I checked the bookshop's new dedicated email account. Curiouser and curiouser. Dozens of emails were already waiting in the inbox. All the enquiries were related to Tom Benchley. Who the blazing hell was this person?

I did the obvious and typed the phrase *who is Tom Benchley?* into Google's search engine. Seconds later I was rewarded with page after page of results.

The answer apparently was that Tom Benchley was a very famous author. 'Well, I've never bloody heard of him,' I muttered, refining my search. Turned out I might have been the only person on the planet who hadn't.

Tom Benchley was world famous for the *Dominion of Gyrth* series of fantasy novels. When he'd initially written them they had made little impact beyond die-hard fantasy fans, but several years later a large American network had bought the rights and turned them into a monstrously successful TV franchise. The books had been repackaged, republished and had sold millions of copies worldwide since the show first aired.

By all accounts, Tom Benchley was a bit of an odd duck. Digging deeper, there was the suggestion of a scandal. Pictures of him falling into a pool drunk at a Hollywood party. Punching a reporter. He'd sacked his publicist, refused calls from his agent, stopped talking to the press and disappeared, before resurfacing in an old mansion he'd bought on the fringes of Upper Finlay. He had barricaded himself away, seeing no one, while everyone waited with bated breath for the penultimate book in the series – which he may or may not have been writing.

The last book in the series to be published, book number four, had ended on a cliff-hanger, leaving the fate of several popular characters hanging in the balance. The TV show, now a cultural phenomenon, had managed to eke six seasons out of the first four books. The producers were now anxiously awaiting the next instalment. It seemed that Tom Benchley had cracked under the pressure.

The murkier depths of the internet suggested he had gone crazy, totally lost the plot. He was said to perform weird rituals on his property. He was living in a fortified bunker. He had two hundred cats. He once ate a live canary.

Tom Benchley's picture was all over the web. He was much younger than I expected, around thirty-five. Meaning he had written the first book in the series when he was little more than a teenager. He was also quite attractive, if you were into haughty features and cheekbones that could cut glass. Very Benedict Cumberbatch, the Sherlock years.

I realised I was vaguely aware of the TV show, but it wasn't really my thing and I'd never watched it. It seemed the hysteria had passed me by. But I was starting to realise that the bookshop's website had shown up on the radar of his rabid fanbase. A random twist of fate brought on by the Google gods. Already, my mind was spinning. Could I somehow use this to help Alex?

Thirty-Two

I hurried downstairs, the beginnings of an audacious idea taking root. I sat in the kitchen, picking at my breakfast. I hesitated for a moment. And then pulled out my phone. Should I do this? Would Alex be mad? My finger paused then I went ahead and texted the gang. I needed more information.

That evening I met with Rosie, Cece, Jim and Noah at the Nelson. We retired to the lounge, packed in tight around one of the varnished pub tables.

'So,' I said, sipping my G&T. I cleared my throat nervously. 'I was hoping to pick your brains.'

'Go on,' Rosie said.

'Does anyone know anything about a local author named Tom Benchley?'

Everyone looked at Noah.

'Why is everyone looking at me?'

'Because you're our resident Gyrthster,' said Jim.

This prompted much laughter and spluttering into drinks.

'Come on, that was years ago! Anyway, so what? I happen to like the novels.'

'Like,' Jim said, raising an eyebrow. 'Don't you think that might be a bit of an understatement?'

'All right, I love them,' he confessed grumpily. 'There. Are you all happy now?'

'He read them before they got popular,' Rosie said in a droll voice, rolling her eyes. 'And don't we know it.'

Jim laughed. 'I remember you running around the local woods dressed as Yorath the Witch Slayer.'

'I was nine, for God's sake.'

'I seem to recall you being a bit older than that, mate,' Jim said, smirking.

Noah took a sip of his pint, blushing furiously. 'Have you really not heard of Tom Benchley?'

I shook my head.

'Come on,' Noah said. 'Death to Fargore.' He contorted his hands into some kind of weird intricate salute. 'No?'

'The people wandering down the street in fancy dress, then,' Rosie said. 'You never wondered what all that was about?'

'Cosplay,' Noah said, 'not fancy dress.'

'You tell yourself that,' Jim said, teasing him good-naturedly.

In truth, there were so many wonderful oddballs

in Upper Finlay that I hadn't been able to separate the native ones from the non-native ones.

Now that I thought about it, there had been this one time when a bloke in full battle armour had come clopping down the high street on an irritated looking horse. But to be honest I thought that was just, you know, standard Upper Finlay.

'Anyway,' I said. 'Back to Tom Benchley. Just how reclusive is he?'

'On a scale of one to ten, that would be an eleven,' said Noah.

'But he must be fond of Upper Finlay at least – if he came back to live here.'

'As I understand it,' Jim said, 'the mansion he owns is where his mother used to work as a cleaner. Sounds more like a way of settling old scores to me.'

Hmm, that sounded less than encouraging. I pressed on.

'So how would someone go about seeking an audience with him?'

'You wouldn't,' Noah said. 'Tom Benchley doesn't do audiences. Nor does he do book signings, public appearances, or anything else. If you tried to get in touch, you'd probably end up with a cease and desist order. One thing he does like to spend his money on is shit-hot lawyers and security.'

'There must be some way of getting in touch,' I said.

'Believe me, Daisy, you'd only be joining the back of a very long queue.'

'Why the sudden interest?' Cece asked, turning to me. 'Are you a secret Gyrthster as well? I hear he's quite dishy.'

'I heard he was as mad as a box of frogs,' Rosie said.

Cece pouted. 'Spoil sport.'

'Yeah, Daisy, what's brought on this sudden interest?' Jim asked.

I gave a casual shrug. 'Just wondered.'

Jim squinted at me. 'I'm not having that. I can see the gears whirring.'

I paused for a few moments, wondering how much I could tell them. I hated going behind Alex's back, but surely they had to have some idea of the hole he was in.

'It's the bookshop,' I said. 'It's in a bit of trouble.'

They all shared a knowing look.

'So you know about that too?' said Rosie.

I nodded cautiously.

'And do you have any idea just how bad it is?' Jim asked. 'Because we sure as hell don't. We've tried to get it out of him, but Alex clams up whenever we mention it. You know what he's like. Happy to help everyone else. But he never wants to accept any help himself.'

'It's bad,' I said feeling like a traitor. 'Very bad.'

A silence fell over the table.

'And how does Tom Benchley figure in all of this?' asked Noah.

'I thought if I told him the local bookshop desperately needed his help, he might consider doing an author event to raise some money…'

Looking around the table, I could see that no-one was buying this idea.

'It sounds stupid now that I say it out loud. But I just keep racking my brains trying to think of some way to help. Even just to buy Alex some time.' I put my head in my hands, close to tears.

'Hey, come here.' Noah said, wrapping his arm around my shoulder. 'Don't get upset. It was a lovely idea. You're a good friend.'

Rosie slammed her glass down, startling everyone. 'Hang on,' she said. 'I've only gone and had a bloody thought.'

'First time for everything,' Jim said. Cece pinched him.

'Shut up, Jimbo. Let Rosie talk.'

'There is one thing, now that I come to think of it…'

Cece abruptly switched sides. 'For god's sake, Rosie – spit it out!'

'It's Liam,' Rosie said.

'Ugh,' Jim pulled a face.

'What about him?' I asked.

'He was going on the other night about this new job he's picked up. Said he was working for a local celebrity. That I wouldn't believe who it was even if he told me. He said that money was no object for this bloke and that he was raking it in.'

'Isn't he a landscape gardener or something?' Jim asked.

Rosie nodded. 'Liam was loving it, though. His little secret. To be honest, he was aggravating me so much I purposely didn't push. But now that I think about it, who else could it be? Tom Benchley is literally the only celebrity I can think of that lives nearby.'

'Oh come on, I bet there's all sorts of famouses living around here,' Jim said.

We went silent for a while.

'Sorry,' Rosie said. 'I tried.'

'Is Liam in here tonight?' I asked, clutching at straws.

'I think I saw him in the main bar earlier, playing the fruit machine,' Noah said.

Rosie shook her head disgustedly. 'That's where half his wages go.'

'Sod it,' I said. 'Let's get him in here and give him a good grilling.'

'I think that's Rosie's job,' Cece said, smirking.

'Ugh,' Jim said.

Rosie pulled a face. 'Do I have to? He already thinks he's got me right where he wants me.'

I didn't feel comfortable forcing the issue, but Cece – God love her – gave Rosie a shove. 'This is for Alex, remember?'

'Fine!' She stomped off to go and find him.

A few minutes later, Liam slouched into the snug, followed by Rosie. We all stared expectantly up at him.

'You wanted to speak to me?' Liam said.

There was some throat clearing and shuffling around.

'Bloody hell. It's like being in court. What am I supposed to have done this time?'

This was my crazy idea, so I guessed it was up to me to follow it through.

'Tom Benchley,' I said. 'We were wondering what you could tell us about him.'

'Who?' Liam said unconvincingly. A criminal mastermind he was not.

Rosie laughed. 'Who! Will you get a load of him!'

Liam looked at her, realising where the tip-off had come from. 'Oh, right, I get it now – you've been shooting off your mouth.'

'Well if you will go bragging about your newfound riches, what do you expect me to do?'

'Enough of the bickering,' said Jim. 'Just tell us, is it Tom Benchley you're working for or not?'

Liam pouted sulkily and stared back at the main

room. 'All right, yes. Are you satisfied? Can I get back to the fruity – it's about to pay out.'

'And you go there once a month,' I pressed, ignoring his question.

Liam nodded. 'That's right. Every last Thursday of the month.'

I counted off the dates. 'Which means you'll be going there in a few days.'

'Well done, gorgeous. There's no flies on you.'

'Must be a hell of a big job for one gardener,' I observed. 'I expect the grounds of that old mansion must be ginormous.'

'You're not kidding,' Liam said. 'But I don't mind putting a shift in for that kind of dough.'

'Still,' I said, 'a little extra help wouldn't go amiss, would it? What you need is a proper crew.' I grinned winningly. 'Us, I mean,' I said, when he didn't appear to be getting it.

Liam stared at me as though I'd lost the plot.

'I don't think so,' he said. 'There's no way I'm putting this gig at risk.'

I leaned forward on my stool. 'This isn't for us,' I said.

'It's for Alex. Remember the other day when you asked me to thank him for you. Actually, thank him "a million" is what you said. You told me you owed him "big time". I assume the van Alex lent you helped you get the Tom Benchley gig in the first place?'

Reluctantly, Liam nodded. 'So?'

'So – you wouldn't even have this job without Alex, right? Well, now he needs you to return the favour.'

Liam shuffled restlessly, wrestling with his conscience.

'I'll make it worth your while,' Rosie said.

'Ha!' Liam cried. 'That's a good one! You're the one who can't get enough of me!'

Rosie drew herself up on her chair.

'Oh yeah, who's the one sending booty calls every other night?'

'Come on, Liam. Help us out here,' I interrupted, before they could get on a roll.

He looked down at the tacky floor, and then up at the ceiling. Finally, he stared at me, shaking his head. 'I must have a screw loose.'

I jumped up. 'Is that a yes?'

'All right, calm down, I'll do it. Now then, Rosie, what was it you said about making it worth my while?'

'Buy a girl a drink first,' Rosie said.

'Ugh,' Jim said, 'you two are the worst.'

That evening snuggled up in bed in one of Alex's old T-shirts, I was feeling cautiously optimistic. The first hurdle, getting to Tom Benchley in the first place, had been overcome. But I still wasn't exactly sure how I could engineer that meeting into an outcome that would produce the kind of money Alex needed.

I started to break the problem down. If, in the extremely unlikely event we did somehow manage to talk to the reclusive author, and even more unlikely, we persuaded him to do a reading, I was sure there would be plenty of public interest. The fans were practically frothing at the mouth for the next instalment, but even if people were willing to cough up a couple of quid, we had a physical limitation as to how many people we could seat. Even if we packed them in like sardines, that would barely cover the cost of the buffet we'd inevitably have to provide.

My brain kept ticking over the problem. We could film the event and sell it. But to who? No, what was needed was a digital annexe to the bookshop which could easily accommodate several thousand more punters. At one time, this would have been impossible, but the technology was not only available now, it was more or less free.

I wondered, could we live stream it, charge for tickets? If we kept admission cheap and by some viral miracle, got the word out, maybe just maybe, we'd tempt a few thousand subscribers. It wouldn't get Alex all the way out of the hole he was in, but it might just be enough to keep the wolves from the door.

Picking up a pen from the bedside table, I started doing the maths on an old envelope and saw that this might actually work, at least in theory. As the numbers added up, I felt a buzz of excitement. Maybe the bookshop could be saved after all. It was a long shot, admittedly, one final straw to grasp. But I had to try – for Alex.

Too het up to sleep, I began plotting my next move.

Thirty-Three

I was a little nervous about revealing my masterplan to Alex. Would he be cross that I'd told the gang just how bad things really were? Maybe he would see it as a betrayal of trust. I swallowed. The thought of Alex being angry filled me with dread.

With my heart in my mouth, I put the laptop under one arm and went into the café where Alex was supposed to be on duty, hoping to kill two birds with one stone. I'd soften him up with the website unveiling before I let him know what he was in for this Thursday. But the closed sign was hanging from the café door and the lights were off in the main room.

I was about to turn around and try the kitchen, when I caught a sudden movement off to my left. A little startled, I looked over and saw Alex flicking the ash from his roll-up cigarette into an empty saucer.

He was sat at one of the tables in the solitary gloom, a printed letter open next to the makeshift ashtray. He looked up and gave me a tired nod.

'Hey, Daisy.'

'Alex, what are you doing?' I asked with a sinking feeling.

He sat back in his chair. 'I needed a moment to myself and the place was empty anyway. It's not like I had to kick anybody out.'

Hearing the strain in his voice, and seeing the state he was in, I decided that now was not a good time to bring up either subject (any subject, really). Stopping where I was, I started to backpedal. 'It's okay,' I said. 'This can wait. We can always talk later.'

Shaking his head, Alex gestured to the opposite chair, folding the letter in two. 'No,' he said. 'It's fine. Switch the lights on. Come and have a seat.'

After a moment's hesitation, I switched on one of the wall lights and went and sat across from him, placing the closed laptop on the table.

Alex stared at it, guessing my reason for being here. 'Have you got something to show me?'

I could tell he was trying to summon some enthusiasm and it hurt my heart that he would be thinking about my feelings even now. *Alex Dean*, I thought, *I'm going to help you whether you want it or not. I'm going to help the hell out of you.*

After a brief pause, I nodded, lifted the screen up,

and turned the laptop around for him to view. A smile spread across Alex's face immediately.

'Bloody hell, Daisy,' he said. 'This is brilliant.'

Pulling the laptop closer, he ran his finger over the touchpad and explored the website in more detail. When he reached the *History of The Bookshop Café* page, his eyes widened. A look of total absorption entered his face. I squirmed in my chair, hoping he liked it.

'I found those photos of your father in the stock room. I hope you don't mind me using them.'

Alex shook his head. 'I've never seen them before. These must be from the early days after he'd just opened up.' Alex laughed. 'He looks so young.'

Alex was clearly moved, and for a time, he said nothing. I had the feeling he was fighting back tears. 'I love it, Daisy,' he said finally. 'All of it. The care you've put into this is unbelievable. I don't know what to say.'

'You don't have to say anything.'

Alex stared at me in that searching way of his, as if he could see my very core.

My own eyes were drawn to the letter he'd folded on the tablecloth. 'You're opening your mail now,' I said. 'That's good. At least you can see what you're faced with.'

Alex looked down at the letter as well. 'There's no way of avoiding this one.'

He made it sound so ominous that a little shiver passed through me. 'Why? What does it say?'

'That I have ten days to pay back the full balance of the commercial remortgage or the bookshop will be repossessed.'

I put a hand over my mouth, horrified, unable to answer. 'Surely they can't do that,' I said finally. 'Not in ten days. Some kind of extension must be possible?'

He shook his head. 'I've had all the extensions they're going to give me. They can do whatever they like.'

Alex was struggling to maintain his composure. I saw that he was close to tears. I took his hand, slipping it into mine.

I took a deep breath. 'What if I told you there was still an outside chance of finding the money?'

He smiled and brushed back my hair.

'You never give up, do you?'

I shook my head vehemently.

'Daisy, I can't raise 60k in ten days. It's over.'

'Okay, listen,' I said. 'Don't be cross, but we have a plan.'

Alex's eyes narrowed. 'When you say *we*...'

'Me, Cece, Jim, Rosie, Noah and, um, Liam.'

'When on earth did you get a chance to hatch this?'

'I met them in the pub last night.'

'Did you now? And where was my invite?'

'Don't be cross with the others. It was all my idea.'

His eyes crinkled up, he looked more amused than angry.

'And this plan of yours? I think you'd better fill me in.'

I told him about Tom Benchley and my madcap scheme.

'I've done the maths,' I said to a very incredulous looking Alex.

'You're just going to turn up outside his property, have him buzz you in, and say "Hi Tom, I know you're a famous recluse who's never seen in public, but I have this one tiny favour I need to ask you…"'

'Nope,' I said. 'I'll be masquerading as a landscape gardener, and so will you.'

Alex snorted laughter. 'Daisy, you're a bloody maniac,' he said.

'So, will you do it?' I asked hopefully.

He looked down at the letter again, reminded of its stark promise.

'I don't know,' he said. 'I love that you're trying, I appreciate it – you – so much, but I feel like this is the end of the road.'

'Don't say that, please. We keep going until the last second if we have to.'

Alex bit his bottom lip, then held both hands up – more a sign of surrender than one of willingness. 'Okay. You win. Just don't expect any miracles.'

I knew he was agreeing more because he didn't want to disappoint me than because he believed in my hairbrained scheme. For once I didn't feel guilty about using his good nature against him. I realised that I had never felt more fiercely determined about anything in my life. I was going to save the bookshop, even if it bloody well killed me.

Thirty-Four

Thursday came around quick. It was the hottest day of the year so far, news anchors across the country rhapsodised from within their air-conditioned studios, not a hair out of place. The same could not be said for me. Alex, Noah and I were squeezed into the back of Liam's van amongst his strimmers, chainsaws, spades, trowels and garden hoes.

I fanned myself ineffectually with my hand. It was hot as an oven. I'd tied my hair up in a messy ponytail, now curls sprung wildly from it, sweaty strands sticking to the side of my face. A trickle of sweat ran down my back and pooled unpleasantly in the waistband of my knickers.

The atmosphere was tense and awkward, and I was starting to regret getting us into this. I guessed I wasn't the only one wondering if today was going to wind up with all of us being thrown into the slammer.

Sensing our doubt, Liam piped up from the front seat as we stopped at a T-junction. 'I can drop you off here,' he said. 'You could walk back to the village in next to no time. What do you say?'

'Just drive,' Alex said, wiping the sweat from his forehead, though he kept staring out the back window as if he wanted nothing more than to follow Liam's advice.

'All right. Just saying. You lot don't seem all that sure about this to me,' Liam said, taking a hairpin bend at speed. I slid down the seat and clunked sweatily into Alex.

Five hot, uncomfortable minutes later, we pulled up to an imposing wrought iron gate, bristling with security cameras. The tense nervous ball in my stomach tightened.

'Take a look at the state of that lot,' Liam said, laughing and pointing towards a huddle of people standing a little way back from the gate. 'Look at him on the left; is he dressed as some kind of elf?'

'A Wyrlon,' Noah corrected him.

'What?' said Liam.

'He's dressed as a Wyrlon, not an elf.'

'Well, whatever it is, he looks a right plonker.'

'You're right,' Noah said, 'he's got the ears all wrong for a start.'

Liam rolled the window down and pressed on the buzzer. He stared down the barrel of the CCTV camera for what seemed like an age before the gates relented and we rolled forwards. Too late to turn back now.

The van made its way down a winding lane, through lush scenic grounds, before Liam pulled into a small glade of beech trees. He jumped out the front seat, came around the back, and opened the door for us. 'Right. Let's get this over with then.'

We all climbed down, stretching out our limbs. As I worked the cricks out of my neck, I caught sight of a large imposing mansion with ivy clinging to its stone facade. A newer annexe jutted out of the back, looking out onto a circular patio and the rolling lawns beyond it.

'Is that the room you were talking about?' I asked Liam.

He nodded. 'Any time I've ever caught a glimpse of Tom, he's always been in there. So what's your plan of attack?'

'We thought we'd play that part by ear,' I said.

'Oh, that's just marvellous. I'm dealing with a bunch of amateurs.'

'We can't all go en masse,' Noah said, ignoring him. 'He'd probably think we were a band of marauding Gyrthsters and call the police. Much as I'd like to meet my hero, I think it should be you, Daisy. You managed to talk all of us into this, after all. Maybe you can work your magic on Tom Benchley too.'

I gulped. He was right, I'd gotten us into this. It was up to me to see it through.

'I'm not sure about this, Daisy,' Alex said. 'I don't want you to get into trouble.'

'I won't,' I said, plastering on a confident smile. 'Right then, here goes nothing. See you all in a bit.' I set off across the lawn before Alex could try to talk me out of it again.

I crossed the patio and peered in through the glass door. I recognised Tom Benchley instantly, although he looked a lot less dishevelled than he had in the pictures I'd seen on the internet.

The author was sat at a huge desk behind an old-fashioned typewriter, although there didn't seem to be much typing going on. His arms were down by his sides, away from the keys, and he was staring blankly at the wall.

I gently rapped on the glass and he half jumped out of his skin, shooting up from his chair. I smiled and gave him a little wave, trying to look as sane as possible. He peered back at me, wondering, I imagine, who the hell was standing uninvited on his patio.

I mimed digging a hole with a spade, which was probably not the best idea under the circumstances. Changing track, I worked a pair of invisible shears instead. Nope, that was worse.

Tom Benchley watched me do this for another

dozen seconds. My plan of not looking like a crazy woman was not proceeding well. Thankfully, I must have looked harmless, because the author's curiosity got the better of him. He approached the double doors and slid the left one open.

'Can I help you?'

My heart hammering in my mouth, I said, 'I certainly hope so.'

He peered over my shoulder uneasily at the surrounding treeline. 'How many of you are there?'

'Just four,' I said.

'So what can I do for you?'

'You're sure I'm not taking you away from your work?' I asked, nodding at the typewriter, noticing as I did so that the paper inside it was blank.

Tom Benchley let out a slightly despairing laugh. 'No worries on that score.'

'Nice place,' I said peering nosily into his study. It was lined with dark oak panelling. Shiny awards lined the walls, next to a picture of him exuberantly hugging Oprah.

'Yes, well, it's far too grand for me,' Tom said. 'And far too big. But you know,' he shrugged. 'Why have money if you're not going to spend it?'

'Hear, hear,' I said, laughing nervously. I got the feeling he was stalling for time. Pleased for the distraction from the non-writing. I wondered how to bring the conversation around to my agenda.

'And what brought you to Upper Finlay?' he asked. 'It doesn't sound like you're a local.'

'No. I'm a cockney through and through.'

'So why Derbyshire?'

Aha here was my chance. *Don't blow it, Daisy.*

'Well, let me see. A few weeks ago I was fired from my job and then I came home and caught my boyfriend cheating on me with this horrible woman called Francesca. After that I got myself into a bit of a state. I don't really remember much about the next part only that I ended up at the train station, got on a random train and fell asleep. When I woke up I was in Upper Finlay. Long story short, now I'm living in a bookshop, temporarily anyway. Which is, um, actually why I'm here.'

Tom whistled, 'Quite the tale.' Then he did a double take. 'Hang on a minute. I thought you said you were the gardener?'

'Well...I didn't *technically* say that,' I replied, wincing. Tom's whole demeanour instantly changed.

'Enough with the tall stories,' he said, his mouth flattening into a thin line. 'You're one of *them*, aren't you?' he said with venom. 'Will you people never tire of hounding me? I'm an author, not a show pony ready to perform on demand. An author,' he repeated, blinking rapidly, his voice rising.

'An artist cannot be expected to turn it on on demand. The blasted book will be done when it's done.'

'I'm so sorry,' I said, backing away.

He peered at me, 'so what are you, a journalist, network executive, a fan – what? Actually never mind. There's only one way to deal with the likes of you.'

He picked up the telephone, a vintage landline with a rotary dial. Oh God, my knees were practically knocking together with fear. This was possibly the worst idea I'd ever had in my life. Alex was going to be mortified, Liam was going to get fired. We were all going to jail!

'Hello Tony, it's Tom. Yes, yes that's all fine. No Dottie's fine. No, she's not been getting at the coy carp again. Tony, for the love of Pete, will you please let me speak? Right, yes, sorry. It's just we've got another one. Over by the beech trees. Well I did try, only you keep interrupting. Right you are. Sorry Tony. See you in a tick.'

Tom slammed down the phone.

'Now you're for it,' he said, stomping across the room and grabbing hold of my arm. 'Come on, move it.'

He frogmarched me across the lawn, over to where the others stood, looking on aghast. This was going about as badly wrong as it was possible to go. As I trotted along beside Tom, I tried to explain myself, but he was having none of it.

'Don't waste your breath, I've heard every excuse

under the sun,' Tom said. 'I really thought I was having a normal conversation for once. But no. Not possible. Everybody wants something from me.'

With a flush of guilt, I realised he was right.

We pulled up in front of the beech trees and I stumbled a little, my arm pinching where Tom still gripped it firmly.

Alex strode forward, removing Tom's hand from my arm and stepping in front of me. Tom Benchley stepped back and looked up. Alex glowered down at him, but he was quite calm when he said, 'I'm sorry that we've intruded on your privacy like this. But touch her again and we really will have a problem on our hands.'

Tom seemed to deflate.

'Oh, who am I trying to kid with the tough guy act. I'm sorry,' he said to me, 'it's the artistic temperament, you know. Mother always said I was a hothead. Let's just wait for security to get here and they can escort you off the premises.'

'So, you won't press charges?' I said from behind Alex's shoulder.

'Not this time, young lady. But be warned, if I catch you on my property again, I will sue you and whoever it was that sent you for every dime I can get.'

To be honest, he was sounding rather lacklustre, as though having wound himself up like a kettle on the boil, he was now running out of steam.

As Tom spoke, his eyes kept drifting over to Alex, lingering on him with a puzzled frown.

'Ah, Tony, there you are.'

Holy mackerel. The largest man I had ever clapped eyes on materialised from behind a flowering hydrangea. He was dressed from head to toe in black, his eyes covered by reflective sunglasses that were almost as shiny as his bald pate.

Tom Benchley glanced at Alex again as Tony advanced, presumably to bundle us into a van with blacked out windows, never to be seen or heard from again.

'Right, let's be having you,' Tony said. I gulped.

Tom held out his hand, looking puzzled. 'Just wait one moment.'

'With all due respect, Mr Benchley,' Tony said. 'I told you I was on my tea break.'

'Yes, yes,' Tom said, 'but this is most peculiar.' He looked at Alex, then back at me.

'You never did say exactly what it is you were doing here.'

'You're right,' I said. 'We do want something from you. But I'm not a journalist or some network executive. I'm not some crazed fan. I've never even read your books.' In my peripheral vision, I saw Tony wince.

'You haven't?' Tom said, looking put out.

'She doesn't know what she's missing,' Noah piped up.

'Quite,' Tom said, slightly mollified. 'So I'll ask you again, why exactly are you here?'

'Mr Benchley,' I said, 'we urgently need your help.'

Tom glanced at Alex again.

'Do I know you? You look ever so familiar.' Then he snapped his fingers. 'Daniel,' he said. 'Daniel Dean, you look just like him. The spitting image.'

Alex blanched.

'You knew my dad?'

Tom's whole face lit up.

'Are you Alex? Daniel's son?'

Alex nodded.

'I knew your father well. Of course, you won't remember me. You were barely out of nappies as I recall.'

'Um, okay.' Tom was only five years older than Alex so this seemed like a bit of an exaggeration.

'Now it all makes sense,' Tom said. 'Your chipper young friend over there.' He gestured in my direction. 'She mentioned Upper Finlay and some frankly odd story about a bookshop. I just needed to see you to put all the pieces together.'

'How did you know my dad?'

Tom sighed, his eyes going misty. 'Simpler times in many ways. We had nothing of course, Mum worked two jobs and still it wasn't enough. Your father, well this is a little embarrassing, he caught me shoplifting one Saturday afternoon when Mum was at work, she was cleaning this place as it happens. Instead of calling the police, he took one look at what I'd snaffled – some utter boys' adventure tosh – and recommended that I try *The Hobbit* instead.

'I'd always been a voracious reader, but that book opened up a whole new world for me. If I'd never read it I doubt I'd be standing here today.' He gestured towards his mansion.

'After that I'm afraid I made rather a pest of myself. But your father never seemed to mind. He took me on quite the journey. Let me read whatever my greedy little heart desired for free.

'Your father was the kindest man. I only wish… Of course the TV show was just starting to take off, so I was in America when he passed. We'd lost touch by then, my fault. I didn't even hear about the accident until I came home and, well honestly, as I'm sure you've heard, I was not myself, shall we say. Still, I should have come to call after everything he did for me. Your father was a good friend. A good man. What a shame,' Tom said, shaking his head.

'Actually, Alex runs the bookshop now,' I said, sidling out from behind him.

'How about that?' Tom said. 'I thought they'd sold it on after Daniel passed away.'

'Nope. Still in the family. At least for another few days.'

That pulled him up short. 'What do you mean?'

'That's why we're here,' I said. 'We would never have intruded on you like this if we weren't totally desperate. The bookshop is in terrible trouble, Mr Benchley, and we need your help to save it.'

'In that case,' Tom said, 'I think you'd better come inside.'

Thirty-Five

Liam was well and truly in the doghouse, so he remained outside while Noah, Alex and I retired to Toms study and drank tea. A fat, massively fluffy cat wound her way around Tom's legs, purring aggressively. I leant down to give her a pet and she hissed at me, bearing fangs.

'Now, now Dottie,' Tom said.

'Err do you have any other cats?' I asked, thinking about the rumours of him having several hundred.

'You're quite enough for me, aren't you Dottie?' Tom crooned. Dottie leapt onto Tom's lap with an audible thump and settled in. He winced as she dug her claws into his thigh and then looked up at him as if to say *go on, say something. I dare you.*

'Tony, be a love and do something about this,' he said, gesturing at the cat. Tony, who had positioned himself by the door like a bouncer at a nightclub, unfolded his arms and scratched his chin.

'Mr Benchley,' the massive man said, 'I'm afraid I'm not insured for that.'

'Fine,' Tom said. 'I'll just sit here and die the death of a thousand cuts, shall I?'

'Yes sir,' Tony said. 'As you wish.'

Having been defeated by his own snark, Dottie remained in Tom's lap, purring victoriously.

'So explain to me again why you saw fit to break into my home and accost me unannounced,' Tom said. I paused and examined his face, but I had a hard time reading it.

'Go on. I'm listening.'

'The bookshop is in financial trouble. It's going to be repossessed unless we can come up with the funds to pay the bank off. We've exhausted every avenue. We just don't have the money.'

'But I don't see how I can help,' Tom said. 'Are you looking for a handout? Because, well, my assets aren't very…liquid at the moment I'm afraid.'

'Of course not,' Alex said. He was looking increasingly uncomfortable and I realised how difficult this whole conversation was for him.

'Not money,' I said. 'Just your help.'

'Go on.'

I took a deep breath. It was all on the line. I'd better not mess it up this time.

'A reading,' I said. 'For one night only. That way I can stream it to your worldwide following and make enough to save the bookshop from closure.'

'I don't do readings,' Tom said firmly, 'or signings, or any other kind of public appearance. Not anymore.'

'But why? Your books are so popular. People love them,' I said.

Noah nodded enthusiastically.

'Not that I blame you, of course,' I continued. 'I expect you're a bit sick of all the adulation.'

Tom laughed unhappily. 'Adulation I'm perfectly fine with, my dear.'

I took a guess. 'Is it the writing? Is it not going so well?'

'This is all rather embarrassing,' Tom said, his shoulders up around his ears.

'It's okay,' I said sympathetically. 'You can tell us.'

'I'm afraid while I was writing *The Dominion of Gyrth* I was going through a stage of taking some rather strong hallucinogenics,' he said.

'Righto,' I replied, for lack of a better response.

'I thought it made me interesting, I suppose. You know, the tortured artist. The truth is, I don't even remember writing the darned things. I mean what the hell are the Children of Punga when they're at home?'

Noah clutched his chest.

'You wrote their entire history,' he said, 'from

the dawning of the golden age to the massacre at Mythering. The rise and fall of an ancient underwater civilisation all in one thousand perfectly formed words.'

Tom shrugged.

'Not a scooby,' he said. 'Now here I am. Stuck. I can't make head nor tail of it all. I can't bear to read them back, it's like hearing your voice on the answerphone. It doesn't sound like me. That's why I came back here three years ago. To get away from all the distraction. Finish the darn books and move on. But I just can't. That's the real reason I've been holed up here.

'Daisy, I'd love nothing more than to do your reading, but the truth is, I've got nothing to read.

'That whole fictional world was created by an out of control youth with a Tolkien fetish and a drug problem. I can't get back into that same headspace.

'I even tried acid again. It did not go well.'

Tony shook his head.

'We will not be repeating that experiment, sir,' he said.

'So you can see my issue. All these endless characters, and royal bloodlines, and what have you, it has so little to do with me. Just today I was reviewing a past scene in which a minor character impales his half-brother or possibly his uncle with a spiked halberd, and I was thinking, who the hell is that?'

'He's the third cousin removed of Wyner Rookstaff,' said Noah, without missing a beat.

Despite himself, Tom Benchley laughed, impressed by Noah's powers of recollection. 'A fan of the series, I take it?'

Noah nodded and gave a nervous cough.

'I loved the books as a kid. I know them like the back of my own hand.'

Listening to Tom recount his troubles, an idea suddenly came to me. 'I might be speaking out of turn here,' I said, 'but maybe Noah could help you find your way back into the storyline? I daresay the whole process would go a lot quicker and smoother if you had a guide.'

Noah nodded. Nodded again. And kept on nodding at the suggestion.

'And maybe in turn you could do a reading. If Noah can help you whip it into shape.'

A little glimmer of mischief lit up Tom's face.

'After what your father did for me, Alex, I feel I have to repay the favour. Besides, it'll drive my publicist mad.' He grinned. 'He's been on my case daily for the last three years. Irritating little twerp.

'Sod it. I'll do your reading. Now hold your horses,' he said when he saw my excited expression, 'I said I'd do a reading of some sort, but I really need to think about whether I'm ready to reveal the new content to the world. When would you need to know by?'

I laughed nervously. 'By Monday.'

'Monday!' he exclaimed.

'We're up against the clock,' I said. 'To stave off disaster, we're talking days, not weeks.'

'Okay,' Tom said. 'I'll let you know on Monday. But I can't promise you anything – you need to realise that.'

'Either way,' Noah said, 'I'll be here first thing tomorrow.'

'No, no,' Tom said. 'That's not nearly enough time. Noah, my love, I'm afraid we are going to have to start right away.'

'Sure,' Noah said, playing it cool. 'I guess I could re-jig my schedule a bit.'

'Now then, if the rest of you are done invading my privacy, it appears to be cocktail hour.' It was ten-thirty. 'Noah, would you care to join me?'

Noah looked like he was about to spontaneously combust with joy.

As Alex and I traipsed out of Tom's study, I was glowing.

'I can't believe we pulled that off.'

'*You* did,' Alex said as I bounced along beside him. 'I just sat there like a rabbit caught in the headlights.'

'The bookshop means everything to you,' I said. 'It's no wonder things have gotten a bit too much. You know, Alex, you don't always have to do everything by yourself.'

Alex took a deep breath. 'I couldn't believe it when he said he knew my father. Dad never mentioned it.'

'I suppose he was just some kid your dad helped back then. Not the hotshot author he is now.'

'My dad was always helping people,' Alex said.

'Sounds familiar,' I said, linking my arm through his. 'I'm not saying this is in the bag. Not by any means. But you know, I definitely think we're in with a chance.'

'Maybe,' Alex said, looking positive for the first time in days.

We approached Liam who was hacking at the hydrangea bush with a pair of wicked looking shears, his face like thunder.

'Well, you didn't get me sacked then with this little stunt. That's something.'

'Exactly,' I said. 'No harm done. So can we have a lift back now?'

Liam tossed his head back and laughed. 'You must be bloody joking! You've signed on as gardeners for the day. The least you can do is pitch in.'

He pointed at several large bags marked *manure*.

'You can start by spreading that lot on the roses.'

Thirty-Six

The next morning, I sprang into action. I'd pencilled in the following Friday for Tom Benchley's reading. That gave me a total of seven days to make this event a reality, raise the money, and have the necessary funds clear. It was going to be tight.

After breakfast, I turned the stock room into a makeshift base of operations, having already cleared the desk of clutter and made room for an office chair. Janice popped in every half hour or so for an update, and to ply me with endless cups of tea and biscuits.

To begin with, I studied the various live streaming platforms, looking for the one that promised the greatest reliability, swift and secure payment, and which could handle the kind of bandwidth that was needed. I winnowed the options down to three, then two, then made my pick.

'Found one?' Janice asked, bringing me another refill.

'Wondercast. They'll live stream the event, we'll sell tickets through their platform, and best of all they come in and do all the filming, production, etcetera, for you. They charge ten percent of the profit, but there are no upfront costs.

'We don't even need any equipment; they provide all that. The only snag is the deposit. It's not much, but it's non-refundable if this all falls through.'

Janice snorted. 'If it means saving the bookshop, I'll pay it.' I leapt up and enveloped her in a hug.

'Are you sure?'

'Anything for Alex,' she said. I knew how she felt.

That was two major issues taken care of, not bad for a single morning's work. But there was no way I could rest on my laurels. The amount still left to do was intimidating. Every second counted.

Next up, it was social media. I set up new accounts on Twitter, Facebook, Reddit, and all the unofficial Dominion of Gyrth forums; everywhere that Gyrthsters congregated online to pore over their obsession.

With Noah's help, some nifty software, and my own intuition, I started to identify the biggest champions and key influencers. Things picked up a notch when Noah sheepishly admitted he was head of his local chapter of Benchley's Berserkers, the unofficial fan club for all things Tom Benchley. The first tendrils of excitement were already reaching out to the fandom. I checked Wondercast. Ten sales so far. Okay, not great, but I had only just gotten started.

I also started tracking down traditional journalists who might be interested in this sort of thing. I collected all this info in a massive spreadsheet, ready to begin my outreach in earnest.

At five-thirty the next morning, I started contacting all the people on my list. At five-forty-five I started fielding irate phone calls from Tom Benchley's publicist. To say that Alan Richards of Alan Richards Inc. was not pleased was a bit of an understatement. But seeing as Tom had repeatedly sacked him over the last few years, he could bluster as much as he liked. I was doing this with Tom's blessing, it was happening. When I remarked that it could only be to his benefit that Tom was actually doing promo again, even though it had come about in a way he didn't agree with, Alan mulled it over for a moment then said begrudgingly, 'You're certainly a pushy young thing. But really you need an expert on the case.'

'Sure,' I said, gritting my teeth. I was willing to take whatever help I could get. Within the hour, Alan had arranged a phone interview with the *Guardian's* entertainment journalist. True to form, Tom was refusing to do interviews; not wanting to dilute the impact, he'd said grandly. So it was down to me. I couldn't give the journalist much, but she seemed interested enough in the fact that Tom was giving a reading at all after so many years. She especially liked the saving the local bookshop angle, which I cunningly managed to shoehorn into the conversation. An article appeared on the website that afternoon. Within a few hours, the post had been shared thousands of times. *All right Alan*, I thought begrudgingly, *you know your shit*. Up went the ticket count yet again.

By the end of the day, my wrists ached from typing and my jaw from talking. There was still so much to do, but one glance at the ticket sales steadily ticking upwards was enough to reassure me I was on the right track.

Just as I was considering a loo break and maybe a quick breath of fresh air, Cece and Noah poked their heads around the door.

Cece laughed when she saw me behind the desk surrounded by dozens of hand-written notes and print-outs. 'You look like a five star general – as if you're waging a war!'

I smiled wearily. 'Well, Sergeant Cece, what news have you got for me from the front line?'

'We spent the day with Tom. I only went for a nose really, but Tom seemed rather keen for me to stay and he's got a pool on the grounds. So…'

'Cece just happened to have her swimsuit with her,' Noah said.

Cece shrugged. 'It's best to be prepared, I always say.'

'And the fact that you haven't read any of his books? I take it that wasn't a big issue?'

Cece pursed her lips and thought it over. 'No. It was fine. I think Tom just liked me being there.'

'Yes for some strange reason he didn't seem too put off by the sight of you swanning around in a skimpy bikini,' Noah said.

Cece pouted.

'It was hot out,' she said. 'You joke, but he is enormously lonely, locked away in that big old mansion.'

'My heart bleeds,' I said dryly.

'Anyway, back to the matter at hand. Noah, how did it go with Tom? What do you think? Are we still on for next Friday?'

'The reading's definitely still on. He's actually quite excited about it. He's got a special piece all picked out. Says it's a surprise for Alex. But he's still anxious about revealing any of his new material. I think deep down he wants to, but it's not easy for him. Honestly right now, I think he could go either way,' Noah said.

'Well, I guess we take what we can get,' I said, trying not to feel too discouraged. 'It's really very generous of him to be doing this at all.'

'I think it's good for him,' Cece said. 'Noah says the writing is really very good. He just needs a push, a bit of confidence. I think all the success and expectation got a bit much for him. He acts confident, but I don't think he is, not deep down.'

'When are you going back?' I asked.

'Tom asked us to come in tomorrow,' Cece said. 'If we can make it.'

'Can you make it?' I asked anxiously.

'Of course,' Noah said. 'If it means saving the bookshop, it's the least we can do.'

It was the second time I'd heard that kind of pledge today. It was lucky that Alex had such great friends, although lord knows he deserved them.

Right, back to work. Things were starting to gather steam, ticket sales creeping ever upwards. We'd had some interest from the local press, and another national newspaper was running a story. They'd even had a lively debate about Tom Benchley on the chat show, *Loose Women*.

The problem was, all anyone seemed to care about was whether there would be an announcement about the new book.

I thought it likely that Tom wouldn't be ready, and the thought was a tight knot in my belly that wouldn't go away. I realised that anything else would be a massive anti-climax. Sure, we might make some money, but I had talked Tom into this, and I felt responsible for any backlash he might face. Even if it was his decision.

On the Monday, I was a bit of a wreck as we waited on the author's decision. Bristling with nervous energy, I went upstairs to see how Alex was doing. We would be hosting the reading in the big room upstairs and Alex had been working on it for the last few days.

When I poked my head through the door, I saw that he'd created something special. The room was not only clean and tidy, with rows of neatly laid out chairs but had a warm and intimate ambience as well. The lighting was just right, dim enough so that everyone would look attractive, bright enough so that we wouldn't have to squint to see them. The walls were lined with quirky paintings from local artists, and the shelves along the edges of the room were bursting with books. Everywhere mahogany gleamed.

Alex was waxing one of the chairs, bringing its sheen out, but stopped when he saw me. He nodded at the room in general.

'What do you think?'

'It's perfect,' I said.

'How are things going your end?'

'Good,' I said. 'A few loose ends, but I should be able to sort those out tomorrow. Now all we need is for Tom Benchley to come through.'

'About that…' Alex said, even now not sounding all that hopeful.

'Still not ready to take a leap of faith?'

Alex smiled. 'I am trying, Daisy.' He put down the waxing cloth and took a few steps towards me. 'To be honest, what I fear as much as anything is that all of this will be a huge disappointment for you.'

Studying his face, I could see that he meant it. Even now, Alex was thinking about me, worried about my feelings.

'It's fine,' I said, trying to speak breezily. 'It's not like I have much of a professional reputation to squander.'

'Still, you are going out on a limb here,' he said.

I shrugged. 'Maybe a little bit.'

'And you're doing it for me,' he said with emotion.

I tried shrugging this off too, without much success.

'That's what friends are for.'

Alex's face ticked. I realised that word – friend – was like a dagger in his heart. But what could I do? I'd made my decision. I certainly wasn't going to keep leading him on. I was busy trying to think of something to say to break the tension when I was saved by the pounding of feet running up the stairs.

Cece and Noah burst in.

'It's on!' Noah said. 'He's going to read from the first chapter of the new book.'

The blood rushed out of my head. Holy shit. The fandom was going to go mental.

I rushed forwards and swept them up into a fierce hug while Alex watched on, laughing. 'You two are bloody marvellous!'

'I think it's Cece you have to thank,' grinned Noah.

'Nonsense,' Cece protested. 'You were the one who helped him out with that knotty issue of Gyndor being his own uncle.'

'Still,' Noah added. 'I don't think it hurt our chances that you agreed to go on a date.'

Cece wrinkled her nose. 'It's hardly a date. I said I would take that great lump Dottie to the groomers with him to get her claws clipped. And maybe we'd get a coffee while we wait.'

'Sounds like a date to me,' Noah said.

Thirty-Seven

The fandom was already bristling with news of Tom's first public appearance in years. But this was going to blow things up. I hesitated to pull the trigger. If it fell through, I'd be public enemy number one. But there wasn't room for doubt. I had to be decisive, there was so little time left.

And so, fingers shaking, I started to type. Thirty minutes later the phone started to ring off the hook. Oh boy.

Of course, the announcement was greeted with scepticism in some quarters. But sceptical or not, with the long-awaited news about the penultimate book in the series finally out there, things really started taking off.

I tracked the announcement over various platforms with the aid of some analytics software. It spread like wildfire, just as I'd hoped, going viral before the day was through. And that was not the only way to judge the success of this promotion. Straight away the number of ticket sales took a huge leap upwards.

Whereas before we'd sold only a few hundred, now it was thousands. And counting. Glued to the laptop screen, my mouth was dry as I watched the numbers mount. I suddenly realised the enormity of what I'd done. I started to shake. What if it all went wrong?

Now that he was fully on board, Tom was making a thorough pest of himself about ticket sales, his ego not happy with anything less than record numbers. Finally, I had to get firm with him, reminding him that he had better get busy writing if he wanted to be ready by Friday. I did manage to wheedle a chunk of money out of him, which when added together with a whip round we did in the Nelson allowed me to put together a fairly substantial digital advertising campaign. Ticket sales crept up yet again.

The night before the big day, I lay curled up in bed checking, double checking, and triple checking my to-do list. As far as I could tell, all the many boxes had been ticked off. Closing the laptop, I lay back against the pillow, looking around the room at all of its now-familiar features. I realised it had morphed into something more than just an impersonal space. I had my own little library of books, hand-picked by Alex, which had appeared one morning with a note that read, *Thought you'd like these*, decorated with a little smiley face.

On my desk sat a framed picture of me and Wolf on the moors, our hair windswept, both of us grinning madly, Alex behind the camera. Then there was Wolf himself, curled up on the cosy dog bed we'd bought for him, snoring gently. For the last couple of weeks, I'd enjoyed joint custody of the Great Dane and had him with me on alternate nights.

The place was starting to feel like home, and yet I was scheduled to leave this Sunday. With all the madness and drama of the last few weeks, that fact hadn't really sunk in until this moment. And as much as I wanted to get back to London, and sort things out with Phil, I couldn't help feeling a stab of regret at leaving this room, and the bookshop, and all of my new friends; Alex more than any of them. In fact, I felt a bit tearful as I switched the lights out and curled up under the sheets, snug in one of his old T-shirts, and tried to get some rest for the big day tomorrow.

Thirty-Eight

Friday went by in a blur as the clock ticked down to seven pm, the hour of the reading.

Outside, groups of people in costume began to gather. The production manager and camera man turned up. Janice helped them get everything ready for the streaming broadcast.

'One less thing for you to worry about,' she said.

'That's brilliant, Janice. Thanks. You're an absolute star.'

She looked at me carefully. 'How are you holding up? You must be knackered.'

'A bit,' I said. 'But it'll all be worth it if we pull this off tonight.'

'Alex is lucky to have you,' she said.

I frowned defensively. 'I'm not sure "have" is how I'd describe it. I will be leaving on Sunday, you know. I can't stay here forever.'

'Why not?' she said. 'I can think of worse fates. And as for London, let it take care of itself, and your crappy boyfriend with it. Better off without him, if you ask me.' Janice was nothing if not blunt.

With nothing left to do, I fussed about the room, straightening the curtains, moving a chair a millimetre one way and then putting it back, trying to keep my nerves in check. When I checked my phone again, it was already five thirty-seven. It felt like time was a whirlpool, speeding up alarmingly.

Tom was scheduled to arrive at six for a brief run-through. Cece had agreed to go and pick him up at five-thirty and calm any last-minute nerves. At five-forty, I went over to the window and stared down at the road, hoping to see Cece's Mini come rolling along it. But as the minutes passed, and six o'clock came and went, there wasn't any car in sight.

6:02, 6:04, 6:06…

With every minute that passed – every second, actually – the sinking feeling grew more intense.

At six-fifteen, I decided to call Cece and see what the holdup was. She answered on the third ring.

'Hey Daisy,' she croaked. Her tone filled me with dread.

'Oh no, what's happened?'

'Tom doesn't think he can go through with it.'

I ran a hand though my hair, panic flooding my whole body.

'But he has to.'

I peered out of the window onto the street. The throng had got bigger. A carnival atmosphere seemed to be building. One entrepreneurial soul was selling dubious looking hotdogs. Another was playing a lute.

'He's an absolute wreck, Daisy. I knew this was going to be hard for him, but I had no real idea just how difficult.'

'Where is he now?'

'In his study, pacing about frantically, breathing into a paper bag.'

Oh God, they hadn't even left yet.

'Put him on,' I said firmly.

Cece hesitated. 'You're not going to shout at him are you, Daisy?'

'Of course I'm not going to bloody shout at him!'

'All right. Just a minute.'

Through the receiver, I heard footsteps, a knock at the door, and then a low mumble. After another few seconds, a man's unsteady breathing.

'Tom, is that you?' I asked as delicately as I could.

'Daisy, I'm so sorry, but I can't go through with this.'

'Listen, Tom, we're all here for you. Me, Alex, Cece, Noah. There's no need for nerves. We've got your back.'

'It's not that,' he said. 'What if they don't like it? What if I'm a laughing stock?'

'Impossible,' I said. 'Would the Elden of Tarf worry about that? Would the fearsome Lady Beaumont? The man who wrote those kick–ass characters should never be afraid.'

'You read my books!'

'Guilty,' I said. 'Meet your new number one fan.'

There was a long pause on the other end of the line.

'You're right, Daisy. The hero must always vanquish his enemy. Fear is my enemy and I must slay it. "Do one thing each day that frightens you," Mother always used to say. Well this ought to last me for a year.'

He was gearing up to make a speech.

'So are you cool?' I hurriedly interrupted.

'As a cucumber,' he answered.

'Great! You won't regret it, Tom. I promise you, we're all here for you. But if you could get your skates on and hop in Cece's Mini, that would be wonderful.'

'Darling, I really feel I ought to have a whisky first.'

'Just the one though, Tom. A quick nip. We need you here in the next ten minutes.'

'Okay. I hear you. See you shortly.'

Putting the phone back in my pocket, I breathed a huge sigh of relief as Alex entered the upstairs room, carrying a tray of canapés. Seeing the flustered look on my face, and the empty room, he put two and two together. The upbeat expression he'd struggled to maintain all week crumpled.

I held my hand up. 'It's okay,' I said. 'Disaster averted. Tom's on his way.'

'You're sure?' he said.

'Positive,' I said. 'I just spoke to him.'

Now it was Alex's turn to sigh deeply. 'This thing has been making me think about my dad a lot. I know it was years ago, but I maybe haven't dealt with him passing as well as I thought I had. We don't always talk about our feelings as much as we should, us men.'

'Well, I'm sure he's looking down on you now and couldn't be any prouder.'

Alex held a hand up. 'Stop it,' he said. 'You'll start me blubbering.'

I smiled. 'Nothing wrong with that,' I said. 'After all, if I hadn't bawled my eyes out when I first met you, we wouldn't be standing here right now.'

'And if you hadn't walked into my life at that point, I'd have lost the bookshop and been out on my ear.'

'You don't know that,' I said.

'I do know that. You're a bloody miracle worker, Daisy Monroe. Don't let anybody ever tell you otherwise.'

I found myself leaning into him, my forehead on his chest. I felt the impression of his body as he rested his chin on top of my head. It felt right. Totally natural. I knew I should step away, but I couldn't.

'We've got this Daisy,' he murmured into my ear.

We both jumped apart as we heard the creak of floorboards behind us a second before the door flew open. It was Geoff and Auntie Lou.

Geoff looked embarrassed, eyes glued to the floor, but Auntie Lou grinned and winked at both of us. 'About ruddy time you two got it on.'

Our guests were starting to arrive.

Thirty-Nine

By a quarter to seven, all the guests had arrived and an air of keen expectancy hung over the reading room.

Outside, a few photographers slouched around smoking cigarettes and drinking the mugs of tea Janice had thoughtfully provided.

The select press I had managed to beg, bully and cajole into attending the reading were already inside, milling around sipping prosecco and chatting to the local dignitaries – the Mayor of Upper Finlay, various members of the Ladies' Guild, The Editor in Chief of the local newspaper. And Auntie Lou.

The camera was set up in one corner, aimed at the lectern, the video feed safely connected. After confirming this for the umpteenth time, I checked the ticket sales again. I did the maths quickly. Holy crapola, even with the ten percent commission we had to pay out, this was going to wipe out a pretty chunk of Alex's debt. This was either going to be an utter catastrophe or an unbelievable success. I practised my deep breathing.

I kept scanning the back street for any sign of our all-important guest. But the longer I stared, the more I started to wonder if there'd been yet another cock-up. Maybe Tom had jumped out of the car at a set of traffic lights, and run for the hills, leaving Cece and Noah stranded in his wake.

The crowd was getting a little restless too, and their sense of expectancy was starting to give way to a few sceptical mutters. But just as I was starting to fear the worst, the green Mini finally turned the corner, whizzed up the road, and screeched to a halt outside the bookshop's front door. Wasting no time, Cece jumped out the car and raced around the passenger side. She held her hand out and Tom took hold of it after a few more hesitant moments. Emerging from the vehicle, he blinked several times into the flashlights of the paparazzi.

Tony made sure the small crowd didn't get too close and Tom chatted with the fans for a moment, signing books and taking selfies. I gritted my teeth and tried not to spontaneously combust from impatience. We needed to start.

Finally, Tom seemed to remember why he was actually there, and he headed towards the bookshop, a little unsteady on his feet.

Rosie and Jim were suited and booted, handing out canapés and some sparkling wine that a local vineyard had given us for free in exchange for a bit of product placement. I reminded the production team to get a shot of the bottles into the stream at some point. Just doing my bit for the British wine industry. I was practically the patron saint of grapes.

Alex and Joe were talking and laughing with an elegant looking woman who I thought might be their mum. I caught Alex's eye and he beckoned me over.

'Daisy, meet our mum, Maria.'

'Hello Daisy,' Maria said with a warm smile. 'I've heard nothing but your name out of these two for the last month.'

Her eyes were chocolate brown like Alex's, radiating warmth, and she spoke with the faint trace of an Italian accent.

'Muuuum,' Joe said, suddenly a little boy again, practically stomping his foot. 'You're so embarrassing.'

Alex grinned.

'I hope these two have been looking after you properly, especially after everything you've done for us. It's really not on that they haven't at least brought you round for dinner.'

Cripes, not another feeder in the family.

'Is he here?' Alex asked, meaning Tom. I nodded.

'Come on Mum, let's get you seated,' Joe said.

'We've reserved you a seat at the front. Guest of honour.'

'Well, it was very nice to meet you, Daisy dear.'

'You too,' I said.

She kissed me on both cheeks, and on a cloud of perfume she was gone.

'Do you want to get the introductions started and put the good folk of Upper Finlay out of their misery?' I said to Alex, conscious that the stream was due to start any minute.

'I'm not much of a public speaker,' Alex said, pulling a crumpled bit of paper out of his pocket.

'You'll do great,' I said, adjusting his lapel.

He looked great too. His tailored suit hugged his broad shoulders and he was wearing the tie I'd helped him pick out. Dark eyes stared back at me, his expression serious, no trace of his trademark smile.

'We've got this,' I said, mirroring his words from earlier. He nodded, took a deep breath and headed for the lectern.

Checking the laptop again, I saw that we were scheduled to start our broadcast in less than a minute and so I gave the sign to start filming.

Alex reached the lectern just as we went live, and tens of thousands of viewers from all over the globe joined us remotely for the event. I could feel the weight of their expectations sitting heavy on my chest. This was it. Tom was here. Against all odds I'd pulled it off. I just had to hold out for one last miracle. Could the eccentric Tom Benchley stay on script, or would this be a disaster of epic proportions? To be honest, I thought it was 50/50 either way.

The crowd quieted as Alex stared out at them. He looked poised and confident, although I knew inside he was a roiling mass of nerves.

He cleared his throat and took his glasses out from his jacket pocket. Putting them on he said, 'Firstly, many thanks to all of you for coming here tonight and thanks to those of you viewing online. Here at The Bookshop Café in Upper Finlay we like to support our local authors. I know it was something my late father took great pride in and I'm glad I can follow in his footsteps tonight. That said, I'm not sure this particular author needs any help in getting the word out, what with him being a household name from Derbyshire to New Delhi, Caracas to Timbuktu…'

As Alex said this, we could all hear footsteps out in the hallway, adding to the sense of drama, and then the door handle started to turn inwards. Taking this as his cue, Alex gestured to the entrance.

'And so, without further ado, I give you Tom Benchley…'

The door swung open revealing Tom, who looked absolutely petrified and seemed rooted to the spot. I could feel my heart in my throat. Was he going to back out at the very last moment?

Cece spoke some final words of reassurance to Tom. Whatever she'd said, it seemed to do the trick. Tom made his way to the lectern, shaking hands with people as he went.

Cece joined me at the back of the room.

'I thought he was just going to have the one quick drink to calm his nerves,' I said to her.

'I don't think that man has ever had just one drink in his entire life. But don't worry. I took the bottle off him after three.'

'Good move,' I said. 'That would have been all we needed – Tom Benchley rolling drunk.'

'Well it would be pretty entertaining,' Cece said, giggling.

'Not what I had in mind.'

She poked me in the ribs.

'He's here now, that's the main thing.'

Tom had reached the lectern, which Alex happily vacated. Now he was gripping its wooden edges, his knuckles bone white. He looked over the heads of the audience, fixing his eyes on the back wall, and for a long time it seemed like that was all he was going to do. Finally, he lowered his chin and made brief eye contact with the front row of guests.

'Hello, Upper Finlay...'

It wasn't meant to be funny – at least, I don't think so – but the whole room cracked up with laughter instantly when Tom said this. It was the kind of thing a rock star might have uttered when greeting a huge stadium audience.

Tom raised his eyebrows, surprised by the response, but also emboldened by its friendly nature.

'Well, I must say it's great to be in front of a home-town crowd,' he said, 'what with me being a native of this fine village.'

This prompted several nods, and more friendly murmurs.

'And when it comes to Upper Finlay,' Tom continued, 'few places feel more like home to me than this wonderful bookshop.'

Again, several members of the crowd nodded, agreeing with the sentiment, spurring Tom on.

'Now I'm sure plenty of you will remember Daniel, Alex's father, who ran this place for many years. And recall his patience, generosity, and incredible enthusiasm for books of every stripe. Well, in my case this meant lending me all the books I wanted, free of charge, knowing how tight money was in our household and what a great thirst I had for fantasy and sci-fi novels. As a result, my imagination had all kinds of strange worlds and universes to feed off. In fact, it's no exaggeration to say that without Daniel's support, the *Dominion of Gyrth* books would never have been written and I wouldn't be standing here before you tonight. Not that that would be a bad thing, necessarily...'

He smiled as the joke landed, and the room echoed with laughter.

'Those of you who have read the third in the series, *Lament of the Blade*, might recall a character called Emil Latvius, the royal librarian who oversees the magical training of Trelawn Rookhope. Well, he was based on Daniel and is an affectionate portrayal of my friend and mentor. And so it is in honour of Daniel Dean, and the bookshop he gave rise to, that I'm going to read this passage about Emil and Trelawn tonight…'

As Tom picked up the paperback, and turned to the relevant page, Alex came to join me.

'Are you all right?' I whispered.

'I'm good. Just a bit overcome by that tribute.'

'Did you know that Emil Latvius was based on your dad?

'Not until right this moment,' Alex said. I slipped my hand into his and gave it a squeeze.

We stood and listened, entranced by the magical world Tom wove with his words. As he finished there was a dramatic pause, followed by thunderous applause.

He waited, drinking in the adulation, nodding and smiling.

'Thank you, thank you. You're too kind. Simply too kind.' Finally, the room fell silent. You could have heard a pin drop. 'Now ladies, gentlemen and

Wrylons,' Tom said with a flourish, 'to finish, I'd like to read you an excerpt from my latest work in progress and the penultimate book in the *Dominion of Gryth* series: *Land of Fire, Song of Hope.*'

Around the room there was a collective gasp. I imagined it echoing through the internet.

I punched the air. *Tom Benchley, you bloody diamond.*

Forty

I spent my last night in Upper Finlay alone with Alex. We sat in the garden eating crisps from a bowl and drinking white wine. Wolf assumed his usual position flopped at my feet, snoring.

The air was fragrant, the early evening warm, bursting with an array of wildlife; chattering birds, pretty jewelled dragonflies and buzzing bees. A cabbage-white butterfly fluttered past, surfing the air waves. I kicked off my sandals and scrunched my toes in the grass. I would miss this.

Although we had lots to celebrate, our mood was a little melancholy.

'So you did it,' Alex said. 'I heard from the bank. We didn't raise all the money needed, but they're willing to take a lump payment from what we did manage to raise. They're suddenly at lot more friendly now that I've got – what did they call it? – a viable business on my hands.'

I bristled. 'It's a bloody brilliant business,' I said.

Alex's phone began to vibrate. He pulled it out of his pocket, checked the display, then stabbed the OFF button.

'Shouldn't you get that?'

'I've been fielding calls all day. God only knows who it was this time – the *Financial Times*, probably. I think that must be the only major newspaper I haven't heard from today. Whoever it is, they can wait.'

'Better get used to it,' I said. 'You do know the world's press is set to descend on the bookshop next week?'

Alex shook his head. 'You've created a monster.'

'Oh, I'm sorry,' I answered. 'My apologies for putting you on the map.'

'It's a fantastic monster, don't get me wrong. I could never repay you, even if I spent the rest of my life trying. All I'm saying is that I could really do with your help with everything that's coming next.'

I stared down at my lap, not knowing how to answer him.

'Website guru, social media ninja, digital overlord – I don't care what title you give yourself,' he continued. 'Just as long as you stick around and help me out.'

Still I could think of nothing to say.

'Come on,' Alex said. 'You are still officially

jobless, at least for the moment, although obviously that's not going to last.'

I shook my head. 'It's not like I did anything out of the ordinary when you get right down to it.'

Alex let out a flabbergasted laugh and leaned forward in his seat to better express his amazement.

'What you did couldn't have been any less ordinary. The bookshop's been rammed all day. The restaurant's booked out for weeks already and other famous authors have been in contact looking to do readings. They're talking about Upper Finlay on the BBC. I've even had location scouts on the phone. Daisy, you didn't just save the bookshop for today. I think you might have saved it for years to come.'

I smiled. 'Well, when you put it like that…'

'Tom's interested in working with you too. In fact, he's giving them no end of trouble. I hear he's refusing to do any more promo unless you're involved.'

This was accurate. Tom had phoned me fifteen times already today in various states of distress, his agent and Alan the publicist had called an additional three times each.

I'd had several enquiries through the bookshop's website contact form asking who'd created the website and where they could be hired. Surely this was everything I'd ever wanted.

My lower lip started to wobble. Not everything.

'Part-time, even,' Alex pleaded. 'Say, three days a week. I know that commuting from London would be a headache, but I'm sure we could work something out.'

It was a headache I could have happily coped with. That wasn't the real issue here. It was Phil. I knew what he was going to say, especially if I was on the verge of becoming his wife. Whatever his plans for our future were, they wouldn't involve me commuting to Derbyshire on a regular basis. And I knew for a fact that he wouldn't be happy about my ongoing friendship with someone who looked the way Alex did.

'It's a lovely idea,' I said. 'And I'm not going to say it isn't tempting.'

'Only Phil wouldn't like it,' stated Alex flatly.

He was only echoing my own thoughts, but still this put me on the defensive. 'We do have a relationship to mend. And it's going to require effort on both sides to set things right.'

Alex slumped, looking utterly miserable. 'Okay. I can see that. I guess it was a crazy idea.'

'Anyway,' I said, clutching at straws, 'it's not like I'm leaving you in the lurch now, is it? I'm sure you'll be able to hire someone.'

Alex sighed. He seemed to be wrestling with what to say next. In the end he simply said, 'Daisy you know how I feel about you. Please stay.'

'I'm sorry,' I whispered, my eyes stinging, 'but I've made a commitment.'

'Can't you just be selfish for once?' Alex whispered. I shook my head. 'I'm being selfish now, drawing this out. Alex, the last thing I ever want to do is cause you pain.'

Hot tears spilled out of my eyes and rolled down my face. I wiped them away.

'Hey,' Alex said gently, 'don't cry. You're the least selfish person I've ever met. I know you're with Phil. It kills me, but I guess I have to accept it.

'I do want you to know one thing before you leave. This is your home whenever you want, or need it to be, and nothing is going to change that. Even if you showed up in a year's time. Two years. Three years. Four.'

A teardrop ran down my cheek. 'Isn't it after seven years that marriages are supposed to run into trouble?'

Alex smiled. 'You're a fast worker, Daisy Monroe. Maybe you can bring the schedule forward a bit.'

I laughed through my tears. 'Oh, Alex.'

'I'm sorry, Daisy. I can't change the way I feel about you, trust me I've tried. If I didn't say something it would have driven me crazy wondering – what if.'

Forty-One

Rodney woke me for the final time. I'd barely slept that night, thinking about what Alex had said. But I was leaving today, and my mind was already half out of Upper Finlay, thinking about Phil. Somehow the thought made me anxious, like I was on a conveyor belt that wouldn't stop. Dragging me slowly towards the edge of a cliff.

Feeling worn and weary and very unsure, I washed and changed and then finished off my packing. I had about three times as much stuff as when I'd arrived in Upper Finlay, but it all fitted into a vintage hold-all that I'd bought from *TCFCTSI*.

My train was scheduled to leave at seven-thirty-two, but I was thankful for the early start as I didn't think I'd be able to cope with any more long, drawn-out farewells. It was the same with this room. I hardly dared to look around me, for fear I'd start crying and be unable to stop.

With my bag slung over one shoulder, I stepped out into the hallway and closed the door behind me for the last time. Then, very quietly, I made my way downstairs to fortify myself with one final cup of tea and a piece of toast.

Entering the kitchen, I stopped on the threshold, stunned by what I found there. Another table and several chairs had been drafted in from the café to accommodate all of the breakfasters. Joe, Janice, Noah, Jim, Rosie, Cece, and even Liam were all tucking into a goodbye fry-up.

Meanwhile, Alex busied himself at the stove, cooking up more sausages and bacon.

Joe laughed when he saw the look on my face. 'And there you were hoping to sneak away.'

'As if we'd ever let you,' said Rosie.

'Not a chance,' said Cece.

I shook my head, trying to downplay the finality of my departure. 'Come on,' I said. 'It's not like I'm moving to the other side of the world or anything.'

'Then why does it feel that way?' said Cece, as the others nodded.

Alex brought a plate over to the table and set it down in front of the empty seat. He tried giving me a breezy smile, although the strain in it was obvious. It was probably for the best that everybody was here. I'd been dreading the actual moment we parted. At least this way, with so many friends present, I could distract myself from the main source of loss.

After we'd eaten, everyone with a car fought for the honour of taking me to the station, but I declined their offers because I wanted to walk and say a proper goodbye to Upper Finlay, the place where I had found so much happiness.

Gathering in the small courtyard at the back of the bookshop, I took my leave of everybody, eyes welling up as I hugged each of them. Finally, it was Alex's turn. The two of us embraced for several moments. He spoke quietly into my ear.

'What I said last night. It still stands. But I know you've made your decision. So I wish you every happiness, Daisy. After everything you've done for me, how could I hope for anything less?'

I pulled away and turned to go before I lost it completely. Then Wolf appeared from nowhere and made his own feelings clear. Taking my vintage boot-cut jeans between his teeth, he tugged at the hem. As gently as I could, I prised his jaws open and finally stepped away. I left to the sound of Wolf crying mournfully. If I didn't get going, I was going to start howling too.

I strode down the back lanes and onto the high

street, my eyes swamped with tears. Every instinct told me to stop. To turn around, but I kept walking. As I passed *TCFCTSI* I couldn't resist one last look at my own personal fashion boutique. There was no sign of Geoff, but Auntie Lou was in her regular spot in the armchair by the window, both feet up on an old leather pouffe. As I shot past, she looked up from her Jackie Collins bonkbuster and offered a sad shake of the head.

Fifteen minutes later, I was on the train to London as it pulled out of the station. My phone buzzed and I picked it up to read a text message from Phil.

Reunited finally! This time there'll be no letting you go!!!!!

He'd sent me dozens of texts in recent days, on a similar theme, all of which seemed to point to an imminent marriage proposal. At any other time, these would have thrilled me. Now my emotions were a good deal more complex than before. It occurred to me that I hadn't checked Facebook once in the last week, weaning myself off Phil's updates completely. Staring out the window, as the dramatic Derbyshire countryside flashed by, I told myself this stood to reason. I'd had no time, thanks to Tom Benchley's reading.

Come on, Daisy. Pull yourself together, girl.

I muttered it under my breath, knowing I couldn't afford to get caught up in two worlds – halfway between London and Upper Finlay. For all my wistful thoughts about what might have been, it was definitely time to commit. Probably, Upper Finlay would start to feel like a dream once I was back in the swing of things. A lovely dream that I'd always look back on fondly, but my real life was ahead of me, with Phil. As for Phil, he was about to give me the clearest sign possible that we belonged together. Maybe his brush with Frannie really had made him see the light. Perhaps things would be different from now on, and not only in terms of him being faithful to me. I was hoping, with this massive commitment, he'd start being a bit more patient and thoughtful as well.

I was so immersed in my thoughts that the journey back was almost as much of a blur as the one that had led me to Upper Finlay in the first place. Still on autopilot, I alighted at Euston and took the tube back to my old neighbourhood, retracing my steps along the high street.

I turned the corner, arriving back on the leafy side street that I'd called home for several years. Halfway along it, I stopped in front of our apartment building, took a deep breath and rang the buzzer.

Several seconds later, I heard the crackle of the intercom, followed by Phil's voice: 'Hello?'

'It's Daisy.'

He let out a raucous laugh. 'What are you doing

ringing the buzzer? You've still got your key, haven't you?'

'Yes,' I said. 'I guess I wasn't thinking.'

Phil laughed again. 'That's my Goose. Flaky as ever. Come on then, up you come.'

Forty-Two

The front door was already open when I reached the second floor. Phil was stood in the doorway, holding it open for me. He looked fit and tanned, bulging with muscles. Seizing me in a bear hug, he lifted me off my feet with a playful growl.

'You've been working out,' I said.

'Every day,' he said, putting me down again. 'It was the only way I could keep my mind off you.'

'I didn't have much time for it myself,' I said. 'Working out, I mean. Other than the odd jog.'

Phil laughed. 'I can see that. You've put a bit of weight on. But that's okay, we'll have that off in next to no time,' he said, grabbing at me playfully. 'I'm going to put you through your paces in the bedroom after all the time you've spent away from me.'

Ugh, why did that thought suddenly make me want to shudder?

Phil studied my clothes, raising an eyebrow as he noted the change. 'I take it this grim northern town wasn't exactly over-endowed with quality fashion outlets. You look like you've gone back to your charity shop days. And what's with that bag? It looks a bit…'

'Retro?' I said.

'I was going to say cheap. But no need to worry about that, I'll take you shopping at the weekend for something new.'

Phil took hold of my hand and started dragging me towards the living room.

'What's the big rush?' I asked.

'I need to get back to the office for a two-thirty meeting.'

Stepping into the lounge, I felt small again, timid, like a paler imitation of the Daisy who had saved the day back in Upper Finlay. The first thing I noticed was a new super-sized TV fitted to the far wall. The last one had been pretty big, and was less than a year old, but this new one must have been seventy inches.

'I splashed out, as you can see. Now you can watch all of your favourite shows in Panoramic Ultra-Def.'

'All *your* favourite shows,' I answered.

Phil laughed. 'Then there's this,' he said, gesturing to a massive white leather sofa that graced the opposite wall. It was another definite upgrade. Sleek and stylish, but with plush cushions.

He watched my reaction, hands on his hips. 'Well? Have I excelled myself or have I excelled myself?'

'Very nice,' I said.

Phil clapped his hands together. 'Right, to business then. Are we going to do this the old-fashioned way? Do you want me down on bended knee?'

To business? What was Phil talking about? It took me a few seconds to understand that he was about to propose. He wasn't even nervous. Despite everything that had happened, he couldn't contemplate me saying anything other than yes.

'I thought we were going to talk about our relationship first?'

Phil gave an exasperated sigh. 'And we will,' he said. 'All in good time. But first let's make this official.'

Getting down on one knee, he reached into his jacket pocket and took out an exquisite ring. Holding it aloft between thumb and forefinger he said, 'Check out this little beauty. 1.13 carats of pure bling, crafted onto a rose gold band. A peerless piece of jewellery. Flawlessly engineered, and with a near colourless diamond at its centre.'

For what felt like an eternity, I watched Phil hold the ring up, turning it this way and that, repeating what the jeweller must have told him. It made him look and sound like a presenter on a TV shopping channel.

I'd dreamed of this moment. But the last month

had changed things. I hadn't known how much until Phil brandished the engagement ring. As it turned out, I may have left Upper Finlay, but Upper Finlay had not left me.

I bit into my bottom lip, then spoke at last. 'Actually, Phil, I don't think I do want you down on bended knee.'

'What do you mean?' he said, looking up at me. 'Oh well I suppose it is a bit corny, but I thought you liked all that romance crap. Here let me just pop this on your finger and we'll crack open the champers.'

'No, Phil. You're not hearing me.'

He looked deeply puzzled until finally it dawned on him that I was turning him down, giving rise to a look of sheer disbelief. 'Is this still to do with the Francesca thing? Because I've already apologised for that.'

'I'm not sure you did, Phil. Not really,' I said. 'But anyway, that's only part of it.'

'Right. I see. Then would you care to tell me what the other parts are?' His voice was becoming more hostile by the second.

'You take me for granted,' I said. 'Always have. This is the perfect example. I told you we needed to talk first, but your whole focus is on getting your own way.'

'But I love you,' he whined. I put both hands on

his shoulders and looked into his eyes. 'No, Phil,' I said. 'You don't.'

Phil let out a bitter laugh. 'Do you have any idea what you're saying? What you're in the process of throwing away? You really want to say goodbye to all this? There's no chance you'll be able to afford a lifestyle that comes anywhere near it.'

'Actually,' I said. 'It turns out that I can fend for myself quite nicely.'

Phil's eyes narrowed with suspicion as something dawned on him. 'Did you cheat on me?' He spluttered disbelief, getting to his feet so that he towered over me.

I cocked my hip, and put my hand on it. 'Not yet,' I said. A vein started to pulse in Phil's temple.

'What the hell is that supposed to mean?'

'It means I say no, Phil. No to your half-hearted shitty proposal and no to you.'

'Please, Goose. You're not thinking straight. You must be tired after everything that's happened. Sleep on it. Give it a day. We can review the situation again in the morning.'

'There's nothing to review,' I said. 'I've made up my mind.'

As Phil realised he wasn't going to get his own way, his whole demeanour shifted.

'Pack your things,' he said abruptly. 'I want you gone. You've got exactly one hour to vacate the apartment. Not that it should take you very long – it's not like any of the stuff in here actually belongs to you.'

'You know what,' I said. 'Bag it and bin it. I've got everything I need right here in my cheap-ass bag.'

'So that's it?' Phil said.

'That's it,' I nodded.

He laughed, his voice dripping with scorn. 'You're making the biggest mistake of your life. You do know I can have my pick of women.'

'You mean like Francesca?' I said.

'If you must know, it's been going on for years, our little dalliance.'

If he'd meant to hurt me with that revelation he'd failed. All he'd done was remove any last shred of guilt I might have felt at rejecting him.

'That says more about you than it does about me,' I said, heading for the door. By the time he had gathered his wits enough to respond, I was already gone.

Forty-Three

It was getting to be a habit, striding away from the apartment after a blow-up with Phil. But this time, I wasn't dazed, I wasn't confused. I knew exactly where I was going. The world, and everything in it, had suddenly become crystal clear.

It was only when I got back to Euston and neared the ticket counter, that it dawned on me that I barely had a penny left to my name. I experienced a flutter of panic. I'd bought a one-way ticket from Upper Finlay that morning, spending the last of my redundancy money in the process. I didn't have enough left to buy a ticket back.

Alex had wanted to give me all the cash he had in the till to tide me over, but I'd refused it on principle. It had felt good at the time, but right now I wished I'd been a little bit more mercenary. I rummaged around in my bag. Maybe there was a couple of screwed-up tenners that I'd somehow overlooked.

Wait, what's this? My fingers brushed against a sealed envelope in the side pocket. I pulled it out and examined it. *Daisy* was written across the front in Alex's distinctive scrawl. Opening it up, I discovered a clutch of twenty-pound notes with a slip of paper wrapped around them. Removing it, I read the accompanying message: *Nice try x*

I realised he must have slipped it into my bag as we'd said goodbye. The sneak. Now I laughed, removing three twenties, and joined the back of the queue.

A half hour later, I was on the train, staring out of the window as London fell away behind me. Thinking back on the last month and everything I'd learned, I realised I was stronger and more capable than I'd ever given myself credit for. I didn't need anyone's help to succeed. I, Daisy Monroe, could do it myself. But I was coming to the realisation that even though I could, it didn't mean I had to.

Just to piss on my self-praise parade, my phone rang. I looked at the caller display and saw that it was Mum. If I had to guess, I'd say Phil had called her with a rundown of the day's events.

'Daisy,' she said flatly.

'Mum.'

'I have it on good authority that you've left Phillip. For good this time.'

I nodded, although there was no-one watching me. 'Yep. That pretty much covers it.'

'He tells me he got down on bended knee and offered to make you his lawfully wedded wife, only for you to throw the ring back in his face.'

'Bit of an exaggeration,' I said.

'But you did say no?'

'I'm afraid so,' I said brightly. Somehow her disapproval no longer seemed to have as much power to wound me. I waited for her cutting response.

Instead she surprised me by saying, 'I saw you on the television.'

'Huh?'

'Oh you know what I mean, the laptop thingy.'

'You did?'

'Yes, well Gerald's absolutely crazy for that Tom Benchley fella.'

Of course he was.

'So when he heard about the book reading, he was all of a tizzy. We could hardly believe our eyes when we saw you there hovering in the background. Gerald's been telling everyone at the club about it. He's ever so proud.'

Bully for Gerald, I thought, but secretly I was a little bit pleased.

'What on earth is going on with you, Daisy?'

I briefly filled her in.

'Well that all sounds like quite the adventure,' she said. 'But where do you go from here?'

'To Upper Finlay,' I said. 'I'm making my way there even as we speak.'

'And what's in Upper Finlay that's worth ruining your marriage prospects for? Would you care to tell me that?'

'Well,' I said, 'I have friends there now, for one thing. Possibly a fledgling career.'

Mum harrumphed.

I hesitated. 'Then there's Alex.'

'Alex...' she said. 'I don't suppose he's that slice of heaven that introduced Tom Benchley last night.'

'Mum!'

'What, darling? I am a sexual creature in my own right you know. My therapist says it's very important that I am recognised as such.'

'Of course, Mum.'

'So you've dumped a sure thing like Phillip, for some...bookstore owner. However dishy.'

'Phil's a loser and he treats me like shit, Mum. Is that what you want for me?'

It was like a superpower I'd suddenly developed – this ability to tell the truth clearly and calmly.

Several seconds passed before she spoke again. 'I suppose not, dear. And this...Alex. He's different, is he?'

'Yes. He is.'

There was another, shorter pause before Mum spoke again. 'Well, all right.'

'I thought you'd try and talk me out of it,' I said.

'You sound exactly like I did when I first met your father. Nobody could talk me around or tell me any different. I only hope you've made a better choice than I did.'

'Oh, Mum. I am sorry that Dad treated you that way.'

'Me too, kid,' she said.

'I have your blessing then?'

Mum gave a sharp laugh, which made her sound more like her old self. 'I wouldn't go that far, darling. I still think you've made a mistake. At the same time, I only want the best for you. Always have. Always will.'

It took me a long while to answer her.

'Thanks, Mum. It means a lot to me to hear that.'

'Yes, well I'd better get on then. I've got to make Gerald his lunch.'

It was late afternoon when I arrived in Upper Finlay. The walk from the train station was as pretty as ever. But it couldn't go soon enough. I was nervous, scared, but there was no hint of confusion. I knew exactly what I wanted. And who.

As I strode along the high street, passing *TCFCTSI*, I saw that Auntie Lou had not moved from her armchair. She looked up from her dog-eared paperback as I walked past and gave me the thumbs up with her spare hand. I laughed, repeating the gesture.

Bloody hell, the bookshop was packed. I could see Janice behind the counter, serving a long queue.

I walked around the side of the building and entered the courtyard behind it. Stepping quietly through the kitchen door, I could hear music coming from inside. I tried the handle and opened the door. Peering through, I saw Alex sat at the table, while he sorted piles of paperwork into neat stacks.

I pushed the door open the rest of the way.

Alex sat up straight, startled. 'Daisy...What are you doing here? Did you forget something?' I could see hope cross his face and he quickly supressed it.

'The position of digital guru,' I said. 'I was wondering if it was still available?'

'Strange as it might seem, I haven't filled that position since the last time you were here, roughly eight hours ago,' he said with a smile.

'Good,' I said. 'Because I'm going to set up my own agency. You can be my first client.'

'And what does Phil have to say about that?'

I stepped fully into the kitchen and closed the door behind me. 'Phil doesn't get a say. Not anymore.'

'Oh?'

He studied me intently.

I stood in the doorway, feeling awkward. Was it possible I had misread the situation?

'Please Daisy,' Alex said, 'put me out of my misery. I don't think I can stand it. Is it just work; do we go back to being just friends?' His face filled with hope. 'Or do you want something more?'

'How can you be so sure,' I said, crossing the room, 'about me, us? After everything I put you through.'

'Because I love you, Daisy,' Alex said softly.

I gave him a slow, lazy smile. 'That's good,' I said and slid into his lap, wrapping my arms around his neck. He pulled me to him, his hands trembling as he smoothed back my hair. I ran a soft trail of kisses across his jaw, his mouth curved up.

And then my mouth was on his, his hand tangled in my hair. Our kiss deepened.

When we finally came up for air, I said, 'Because, Alex Dean, I bloody well love you too.'

About the Author

Gracie loves to create strong, quirky heroines and hopes to introduce you to your latest book-boyfriend crush.

She makes her home in the stunning Peak District in Derbyshire. Where she lives with her partner—amid ongoing negotiations over the size of her book collection and whose job it is to take out the bins!

Get all the latest news from Gracie Player:

Printed in Great Britain
by Amazon